TIMING THE TIDES

Cindy,
Best Wishes,
Cali 2017
LE #23/50

TIMING THE TIDES

A Tale of Love Sparked on the Titanic,
Rekindled a Century Later

CALI GILBERT

This is a work of fiction. Names, characters, places, and incidents either are the product of the author's imagination or are used fictitiously, and any resemblance to actual persons, living or dead, business establishments, events or locales is entirely coincidental.

TIMING THE TIDES

ISBN-13 978-0692859896
ISBN-10 0692859896
Library of Congress Control Number: 2017904331
First printing April, 2017

Serendipity Publishing House
Santa Monica, CA ♥ Coronado Island, CA

Cover design by Cali Gilbert using photographs courtesy of Cali Gilbert, Brian Lippe and Dannyqu
www.flickr.com/photos/dannyqu/14308867456

Edited by Marlene Oulton, www.marleneoulton.com

WWW.CALIGILBERT.COM

For William

"There is a tide in the affairs of men, which taken at the flood, leads on to fortune. Omitted, all the voyage of their life is bound in shallows and in miseries. On such a full sea are we now afloat. And we must take the current when it serves, or lose our ventures."

- Shakespeare

PREFACE

Have you ever visited a place for the first time, yet felt as though you had been there before? Have you ever met someone for the first time, yet felt so comfortable in their presence, you felt as though you somehow knew them? Have you ever experienced dreams that seemed so real you could swear you were actually there? Well, the story in the pages before you follows the parallel journeys of four individuals through two periods...yet they are separated by a century.

In 1912 Bridget McAdams and George Baxter had no idea where life would take them once their paths crossed. Although young adults at the time, they had both envisioned their ideal lives and set out to create them. It wasn't until a fateful day in April that everything changed.

For free spirits, Lily Taylor and David James, the year 2012 represented much more than the one hundredth anniversary of *Titanic's* sinking. Little did they know that a chance encounter would turn their lives upside down and reveal more questions than answers. What would you do if you were given a second chance at life and love?

CHAPTER 1

Lily

Los Angeles, California
March, 2012

Darkness filled the night sky, and the air was so cold my mind escaped its grasp to avoid acknowledging the painful numbness of my limbs. The repetitive swaying back and forth from the waves below the boat had become part of my consciousness, yet the constant screams that filled my senses were becoming unbearable. I wanted to help, but didn't know how. I sat there, completely in a state of stunned shock, surrounded by others who must have felt the same. I closed my eyes and tried to envision a happier place, far away from my current circumstance. I envisioned a warm sunny meadow filled with lavender, chirping birds, and a sense of peace. I imagined my loved ones laughing and all the cares of the world vanishing before us. I was happy. I was safe.

Suddenly I was startled back to reality by a loud thump. I opened my eyes to find a large cake of ice had bumped into our boat. It was bobbing up and down and would certainly slam into the side where I was sitting once again. I gazed out at the sea before me with a feeling of sadness yet relief. I was alive and there were so many who weren't as lucky. My eyes caught hold of a familiar woman from my village, standing on the deck of the large ship with her four small children clinging to her dress. They were doomed to go down with the ship and I was left feeling helpless. Desperation filled my being and I cried out in what sounded like a whisper, yet with every ounce of my strength I yelled, "I'm sorry! I'm sorry!"

****

Just then the door flung open. "Lily! Wake up!" My roommate Kate stood in the doorway looking at me.

"You're late for work AGAIN!"

I sat up in bed, rubbed my eyes and looked at her with what must have been a blank expression on my face.

"You were having that dream again, weren't you?" she asked.

I looked around the room and replied, "Yes, but this time it just seemed so real."

I rubbed my eyes again and then rose from the

bed. Quickly showering, I threw on my favorite pair of black yoga pants and a white t-shirt, pulled my long blonde hair back into a ponytail and headed off to work.

As I locked up my bicycle outside the offices of the *Westside Dispatcher*, I heard someone grunt behind me.

"Morning Taylor! You're late... AGAIN!"

It was Mr. Tillman, my boss, or should I say, boot camp tyrant. He was a fierce older man, tall with broad shoulders and a receding hairline, who was set in his ways and didn't appreciate tardiness.

"Couldn't be helped, Mr. Tillman, but I'm here now."

He grimaced with disapproval, then motioned with his right hand for me to go inside.

The *Dispatcher* was the local newspaper serving the communities of Malibu, the Pacific Palisades, Santa Monica, and Venice on the west side of Los Angeles. I was the staff photographer and for the most part I enjoyed my job. My dream was to write for the paper, but my photography skills had gotten me in the door. Finding this job after graduating from USC's Journalism program seemed the perfect opportunity to do what I loved and get paid for it. There was always something going on around town and I was usually right there to capture it with my trusty Canon digital camera.

In addition to taking photos, I loved being around people and we had our share of eclectic characters here on the west side. Ranging from the roller-blading grandma to the acrobat who enjoyed showing off his balancing acts on the rails of the Pier, it was certainly never dull. I enjoyed living in Santa Monica because of its diversity, and the world of characters who flocked here from around the globe. Our neighboring cities of Venice, the Palisades, and Malibu were equally appealing, each with their own unique vibe that attracted a select group.

After graduating from USC I had found a great house to share in Sunset Park, the southeast part of town near Santa Monica College. I loved being able to ride my bike everywhere or walk to the beach which was a mere twenty-five minutes from my door to the sand. Main Street was always filled with action and the *Dispatcher's* office was right off Ocean Park Blvd., the main drag that stretched from the ocean to West LA. I felt as though I had the entire world at my doorstep, and for this beach girl, that was heavenly.

Once settled at my desk I went over my files of photographs I had downloaded from my camera to my computer to see which ones would work best for the next issue.

"Taylor! You're at the Pier today," Mr. Tillman's voice boomed from the next room.

Every summer during the first week of June, Santa Monica hosts its annual Paddleboard Races. The best swimmers and paddlers from around the globe convene on the beach just south of the Pier for a full day of activities. Several new events were being added this year, and ranged from Stand-Up Paddle and Paddleboard Long Course, Elite Long Course, Two-Mile Fun Paddle, a Paddle Cross, as well as a One-Mile Ocean Swim, Youth 250 Meter Swim, and a Lifeguard Dory Race. Today the media was invited down to the Pier for a preview of what was in store for this year's event. Several of the top athletes were going to be there to demonstrate the new events added and help promote them.

After picking up my assignment list, I boarded a black SUV with my colleagues and we headed down to the Pier. My job was to capture the starts of each race and also get images of the athletes with the city officials and VIPS on hand. Also slated for the day was the announcement of the building of the Surf Museum which would be located on the Pier and contain artifacts dating back to the 1930s. We first met at a stage area on the Pier where the athletes were introduced and a question and answer session followed. Then we headed down to the water. Everything was going smoothly until I was in the water awaiting the firing of the starting gun for the Ocean Swim.

As the swimmers lined up at the starting line, I felt the waves crash against my feet even though I was standing in very shallow water. I wanted to get a good angle from which to shoot, and the tides had shifted by the time the practice races had begun. As I raised my camera and positioned myself to capture the first initial shots, I suddenly began hearing soft murmurs in the distance. I didn't think much of it as I turned around to look out at the sea. I turned back around just as the starting gun went off and snapped the shots I had been hoping to get.

Once all of the swimmers were in the water I began to head back towards the shore when the murmurs returned. I looked back to the sea when suddenly visions of my dream flashed before my eyes. I tried to shake them off, yet they persisted.

"Lily! Are you okay?" asked Jake, one of my colleagues.

I fiercely nodded my head and then replied, "Um, sure."

We headed back up the beach towards the finish line where I needed to capture a few more photos. I took a deep breath and tried to compose myself. I wasn't okay and now I was beginning to wonder what this dream was trying to tell me.

Once we were back in the office I began sorting through the photos I had captured. With each that came up on the screen, an image from my dream accompanied it in my mind. I couldn't concentrate and I was getting frustrated. I continuously rubbed my eyes and tried to shake the images from my mind.

"We're on a deadline here Taylor! Hurry it up!" Mr. Tillman shouted from his office.

I scrambled to organize the photos I thought he would approve and then sent them to him via the paper's shared Dropbox file.

"WHAT THE HELL? TAYLOR, GET IN HERE!"

A look of horror must have come over my face as I sat straight up in my chair. I got up and walked into Mr. Tillman's office only to find him with both hands over his face when I arrived. When he lowered his hands, his face was a beet red and I swore one of the buttons from his embarrassingly tight shirt was going to pop off at any second.

As I stood in the doorway, he motioned for me to

close the door behind me. I sat down and quickly asked, "What's wrong?"

He turned his laptop around so I could see what he saw on the screen. To my utter disbelief I viewed the file I had sent to him. It wasn't the photos I had shot from the event earlier in the day. It was a group of photos from Kate's birthday party. Somehow I had selected the wrong file from my desktop in my frustrated state, and now Mr. Tillman was looking at birthday photos from our crazy adventure in Vegas. Apparently not all things that should stay in Vegas, do. AH! The sheer terror I felt in that moment. Now my hands were covering my face.

As I sank deeper into the chair and tried to think of something to say, Mr. Tillman rose from his desk.

"Taylor, are you happy here?" he asked.

"Why, yes sir, I am."

He began pacing back and forth rubbing his head with his right hand. I had a bad feeling of what was coming next, but wasn't prepared for the reality.

"The last few weeks you've been off your game, Taylor. I'm not quite sure what's going on, but I've made a decision. You're always claiming you want to write for this paper, yet you've barely scraped through your photo assignments of late. I'm just not sure it's going to work out."

I stood up wanting to offer an apology and express how I would do better and something like this would never happen again, but I never got the chance. Just before opening my mouth, Mr. Tillman spoke those words that no one ever wants to hear.

"Sorry Taylor, but YOU'RE FIRED!"

The next few moments were a blur as I left his office. After clearing out my desk and placing everything into a box, I unlocked my bike, balanced the box on the seat and walked home. I still couldn't release the images of the sea and the visions of my dream from my head. Yet now those images were accompanied by Mr. Tillman's expression of disbelief that I would be so stupid as to send him the wrong file. Three years of my life went down the drain in one quick blow. My dream of becoming a successful newspaper reporter was also gone. "How could this be happening?" I asked myself as I unpacked the box of my belongings in my room once I reached home. I had a mystery on my hands that needed solving. I sat at the desk in my room and tried to figure out the occurrences from the last few weeks. When did the dream begin? What triggered it? What was the significance of water? These were questions I asked myself and was determined to find the answers.

The one question that seemed to demand the most attention from me was the one about water. Ever since I was a child I'd always had this love/hate relationship with the sea. Every place I'd ever lived had been near a body of water, whether a bay, lake, or the ocean. I'd always felt as though I needed to be near the water, yet I would never actually swim in any of them. I had a hidden fear of what lay beneath on the ocean floor. I would sit near it, even dip my toes in as the waves crashed along the shoreline, but never swam in it. It wasn't that I was afraid of swimming, or couldn't swim. I was fine in pools, probably because I could see the bottom. There just seemed to be something blocking me from exploring the sea and I could never figure out what it was.

As I sat there contemplating what to do next in terms of finding work and uncovering this mystery of the sea, I knew I needed to find answers, and somehow I had a feeling I wouldn't find them here in Santa Monica. I needed a fresh start, someplace different, a new beginning. I was twenty-five now and felt a fresh start was perfect for this next quarter of my life. Over the last few years, since leaving university, I had always found myself heading down to San Diego whenever I wanted to get away. I loved spending time on Coronado, the small stretch of land across the bay from downtown San Diego. It was a great place to unwind and take time to think, which was what I really needed right now. Plus, what better place to go to uncover my fears of the sea than a place completely surrounded by water? Coronado Island, as it's commonly known, is not technically an island in the traditional sense of the word. It sits on the Pacific Ocean with Glorietta Bay and San Diego Bay to the south and east. I felt this was the answer. Now I needed to figure out a way to make my visit there happen.

As luck would have it, I had many friends in the San Diego area, so I decided to reach out to a few of them about the possibility of moving there. One worked for the local newspaper on Coronado and suggested I could lend a hand there part-time as a photographer until I could find something more permanent. I had saved up enough funds to hold me over for a few months, so I knew I would be okay. The timing actually worked out great because our lease here on the house in Santa Monica was up at the end of the month and I knew Kate was hoping to find a place of her own so she and her boyfriend could have more privacy. I knew she would be okay with my leaving.

Kate had spent the previous night at her boyfriend's apartment in West Hollywood, so when she came back I shared the news.

"You did WHAT and you're doing WHAT?" she asked.

"Yep, I got fired and I'm moving to Coronado. I know it may sound absolutely crazy, but I need to do this for me. You know these dreams have been freaking me out, and I need to find answers."

She didn't reply yet shook her head in agreement.

"When are you leaving?" she asked.

"End of next week."

Somehow she understood and offered to help any way she could. We did at least get a good laugh over the expression on Mr. Tillman's face when he saw the Vegas photos.

The next two weeks were spent sorting through my belongings and parting with things that simply didn't serve me any longer. I went through my file cabinets and found I still had papers from school. I sorted through all my clothes and filled bags to give to the Salvation Army. I completed a massive purge and it felt good. I was ready for a fresh start, in a new city. I was ready to reinvent myself. After all, I was now an adult and on my own. My family lived in New York and my parents were busy putting my brother and sister through school. They had their hands full, but I didn't mind their lapse in communication sometimes. I enjoyed my independence and had become accustomed to it since living in California for the last seven years.

Moving day sprung upon me faster than I had anticipated, and although there was a lot to do, I knew I would manage. Kate had helped me pack my things before heading out of town with her boyfriend. I had hoped to find some other friends to help me pack the moving truck, but no such luck. "No worries," I thought. "I've got this." I had rented a ten foot moving truck and started placing items inside first thing that morning. As I was placing some boxes in the truck, I heard a voice call out from behind me.

"Need some help?"

It was my neighbor, Ben.

"Oh hey Ben!" I replied. "Just with the big things if you don't mind?"

He smiled and said, "Sure thing!"

He helped move my bed, desk, and a couple small tables. The rest were mostly small boxes and I managed just fine.

It was noon by the time I wrapped up the packing of the truck. I then pushed the keys to the house through the mail slot for Kate and hit the road. The drive down the 405 wasn't too bad once I passed the exit for Long Beach. I made decent time and arrived in Coronado about three hours later. I had been able to find a great apartment close to the Ferry Landing thanks to my colleague Jake from Santa Monica. His cousin Mike was a realtor in San Diego and I really lucked out. He also met me at the apartment and helped me unload the truck which was a huge help.

As the sun began setting I stood on my balcony overlooking the Bay, took a deep breath and said, "Well Lily, this is it. New beginning!" I smiled as I was excited about what could possibly lie ahead. I had no idea what that might be, but I was ready for anything.

CHAPTER 2

Bridget

Queenstown, Ireland
April, 1912

With my clothes spread over the bed and the suitcase open, I neatly folded each piece and placed them inside.

"Bridget Rose! What on earth do you think you are doing?" asked my mother as she entered the room.

"Sorry mother, no time. Need to pack!"

Eyeing me with a look of curiosity and concern, she walked over, grabbed my neatly folded skirt from the suitcase, and threw it into the air.

"I see. And where exactly are you going?" she asked.

"America!" I replied.

"I've loved being here mother, but it's been several months since I've seen my beloved Robert and I miss him so. I need to return home." I hurriedly finished my packing so I could travel down to the dock to depart.

Robert was my fiancé and lived in New York, USA, and I was anxious to get back to him. Mother knew of my spontaneity so didn't argue with me. Instead, she kissed my forehead and delivered a warm embrace before allowing me to return to packing.

Although I was born in Ireland, I had been living in America with my aunt Meg for the last five years. I had always had an adventurous streak, and when the opportunity arose to cross the Atlantic, I jumped at it. I had created a good life for myself there and worked hard at odd jobs over the years. Robert was English from London and we met through my cousin Henry. They both worked at Brown and Sharpe, a New England company that specialized in manufacturing fine precision tools. When he proposed marriage last summer, I was thrilled. Now twenty-five, I was eager to begin the next chapter in my life. We've made plans to marry in August in New York. I had been visiting my family since the autumn as my sister, Beatrice had been preparing to marry her long-time beau, John. They had married in March and it had been a lovely ceremony. I returned to Ireland not only for my sister's wedding, but also to share the news of my engagement and decision to permanently live in America. I was happy to be able to return to my place of birth for a while, but now it was time for me to prepare for my own wedding.

The big news around town was the upcoming departure of the luxury liner, *Titanic* which was making its maiden voyage across the Atlantic Ocean. *Titanic* was to begin its voyage to America from Southampton, England, on April 10th, and was slated to arrive in Queenstown, in the County of Cork, around noon on April 11th. Anxious to return to America, I had managed to purchase a third class ticket for £7, 15 shilling. I was meeting two friends, Helen and James, who lived in the neighboring town and we were going to be sailing together on that beautiful ship. We had known one another since childhood, and they were also planning to marry and begin a new life together in America.

The news of *Titanic's* upcoming voyage had taken over the town and flocks of people headed down to the docks in hopes of catching a glimpse of the magnificent vessel. The dock at Queenstown was much too small to accommodate such a large ship, so the *Titanic* had to dock some two miles offshore near Roche's Point. Two tenders, named *America* and *Ireland,* were then used to transport passengers to the ship. This wasn't the first time I had travelled on a ship, as I had taken the *Lusitania* from America to Ireland last summer when I travelled back home. I was excited, however, about travelling aboard the *Titanic*, as it had been referred to as being quite magnificent, even unsinkable.

As I approached the dock area I spotted Helen and James.

"Bridget!" yelled James, as he waved his arm in the air. "We thought you weren't coming."

"Why are you so late?" asked Helen.

"I'm sorry. I hadn't informed mother of my plans, so it took a little longer than I anticipated explaining why I needed to leave so quickly. All is well now, however, so let's go."

We boarded the *America* which would take us across to the *Titanic*. In addition to the two tenders, there were also smaller vessels, called bumboats that carried out sellers of Irish lace, china and other souvenirs to the big ship.

We boarded the *Titanic* via the E-Deck which was the fifth deck below the lifeboat deck. There we were greeted by a medical officer. He was making sure that no one with any health issues boarded the ship as that would prevent them from entering America. Once we were cleared by the officer, we then had to show our ticket and have it stamped. Next we were issued a section number to help us locate our berths two decks below, and there was a steward present to assist in directing us to the proper place. The single women and men occupied opposite ends of the ship. Helen and I were directed towards the stern end of the ship while James was directed towards the bow. We agreed that after we had settled into our respective cabins we would meet up on the C-Deck promenade at 1:30 pm just prior to departure.

Upon entering our cabin we found two sets of bunk beds, a small water basin between them with a small mirror hanging above it, and two White Star Line towels which hung from silver hooks on either side. Our roommates hadn't arrived yet, so we had some room to spread out our things and organize our belongings. The cabin was next to the boiler rooms and we spotted a few sailors walking around as we were being led there. One of them caught my eye and smiled as he passed me in the hallway. He had the most piercing blue eyes I had ever seen. I laid out my evening attire on the bed and placed my favorite book underneath my pillow so I could have it handy for later. Helen pulled out a light blue pastel gown with a stunning draped neckline and held it up.

"Like my new dress?" she asked.

"It's lovely," I replied. "Is it a Lucile?"

Helen laughed and whispered, "I wish."

Hanging it up I shared, "Be careful what you wish for. You know I heard Lady Duff Gordon was aboard this vessel and she now has a clothing salon in New York. Perhaps we shall become great friends one day and we'll both be wearing her gowns to fancy New York parties!"

Helen laughed even louder as we continued to sort our belongings.

Once we had finished unpacking we headed up to the promenade deck to meet James. The sound of a bugle playing at 1:00 pm announced dinner to the passengers. There were three meals offered daily as well as an afternoon tea. I was looking forward to savoring the many selections from breakfast, dinner, and supper each day of our voyage. Many were headed to their respective dining areas, each designated by class. We would eventually follow, yet we lingered as we wanted to be outside to watch as we departed the waters of Queenstown. There was a large group who had the same idea and we were entertained by one of our fellow passengers who played his uilleann, a set of Irish bagpipes, as the engines began to stir. It was a nice send off, yet somewhat sad as the tune he played was *"Erin's Lament,"* the same tune he played on the tender as we were making our way out to the great ship. Part of me was sad to leave my family, yet the part of me excited to return to my Love outweighed the sweet melancholy that lingered after the last note was played.

The *Titanic* was a fine looking vessel and its size truly magnificent. Although our berths were located on the Lower Deck, we were able to venture about some of the other decks that housed accommodations for our class. The F-Deck (Middle Deck) housed our dining saloon amidships where we would retreat to once we left port to enjoy our first meal. Above that on E-Deck (Upper Deck) one would find "Scotland Road," a long pathway that reached from one end of the ship to the other. We decided upon this area as our meeting place since James' berth was located on the opposite end of the ship as ours. D-Deck (Saloon Deck) housed the First and Second class saloons, but also an open area for those of us with Third Class (Steerage) tickets. Finally, the C-Deck (Shelter Deck) housed most of the general accommodations for our class, including a General Room, Smoking Room, and the Promenade.

Dinner was scheduled daily from 1:00 pm - 2:30 pm, and a bugler would play the song, *"The Roast Beef of Old England"* to summon everyone to their respected dining saloons. Our dining room took up a large space and according to one of the stewards, actually consisted of two rooms separated by a watertight bulkhead. We were informed there were two sittings as the space only held slightly under five hundred people and there were over seven hundred of us in steerage. We chose the second sitting so that we could spend time on the promenade waving to the onlookers as we departed. Once we arrived we found a room filled with wooden chairs around long tables that accommodated twenty people each. There were hooks on the walls where we hung our coats, hats and scarves.

After finding a place to sit we enjoyed a lovely meal consisting of Bouillon soup, roast beef with brown gravy, green beans and boiled potatoes. We also enjoyed cabin biscuits, bread, prunes and rice. Between bites, Helen and I conversed of our excitement for the voyage and what lie ahead for both of us once we reached America. I was excited about returning to my Robert. I hated being apart for so long, but wanted to be there for my sister when she married John, and also spend time with my family who I hadn't seen in quite some time. We also had a chance to converse with some of the other passengers as well. There was a young girl sitting across from me named Anne. She was a few years younger than me and visiting America for the first time. I assured her she would love it and she returned my statement with a shy smile.

Following dinner we decided to head back to the promenade. I loved listening to the sound of the waves crashing below as the afternoon progressed. I could easily envision myself sitting here for hours reading and soaking up the sounds that filled my senses. I grew up near the River Lee as my father was a fisherman, and I remembered my younger days swimming and feeling almost one with the water and that which inhabited it. I suppose that was also why I was anxious to get back to New York. Although it was a fine city with so much to see and do, I was also surrounded by the waters of the sweet Hudson River.

As I sat on the promenade with my book, Helen and James decided to go for a walk and check out the other areas of the ship. There was quite a bit to see, yet I was happy with getting lost in the pages on this first day at sea. I was reading *The Story Girl* by L.M. Montgomery. I was excited about reading this book as I had almost devoured the author's *Anne of Green Gables* series when the first books had come out a few years prior. I have always loved to read and could spend hours lost in other worlds, always excited to discover what would happen next. I loved following Anne's adventures in the books and felt somehow drawn back to my own childhood when reading them.

In the stories, Anne Shirley is an orphaned girl who is adopted by an older brother and sister in Prince Edward Island, Canada. I often imagined what it would be like to visit such a place, so close to the shores of New York, yet so far at the same time. When *The Story Girl* had come out last year I was quick to retrieve a copy. I had initially intended on reading it aboard the *Lusitania*, but that wasn't the case. Once I returned home I became busy with helping Beatrice prepare for her wedding and picked up other books to read along the way. So now with several days of time on my hands, I thought it was the perfect opportunity to commence reading this much anticipated novel.

Although the day had brought about clear blue skies, the temperatures on the open sea began to drop as the afternoon passed. After about an hour I felt a chill and thought it best to retreat to the inner accommodations of the ship. I met up with Helen and James in the General Room where they had struck up a conversation with another couple. They had four small boys who had gathered on the floor next to their parents.

"They're exhausted," said the mother. "They must have run the entire length of the ship exploring."

I smiled thinking of Robert and our life together that awaited us upon my arrival in New York. We both wanted children and I envisioned them running and playing in a house filled with love and laughter.

Helen and James, on the other hand, weren't sure

about starting a family straight away. They both loved adventure and wanted to travel. They would settle in New York after their wedding and save up their earnings for a year before exploring America. In a way I was a bit envious as my spontaneous streak wanted to join them, but I knew I was making the right decision. Robert had been working hard for years and I knew how much he wanted a family and to have a home of our own. He had also been so patient with me being away for so long, that I somehow felt I owed it to him to return as soon as possible and become a dutiful wife.

Before long it was time for supper and the announcement came for the two sittings available in the saloon. The first was at 6:00 pm, and the second at 6:45 pm. The family chose the first as the children were hungry and they wanted to retire early. We chose the second and continued chatting until it was our time to eat. We then headed to the saloon where we found a place to sit and enjoyed our simple meal of gruel, cabin biscuits, and cheese.

Once again we met and conversed with fellow passengers. I love to talk and have no problem starting a conversation. Before we knew it we were all laughing speculating who was on board and what life must be like for those in First Class. Helen and I felt very blessed knowing how fortunate we were to be aboard this ship, heading to America to begin lives with the ones we loved. We knew many from our class were immigrants heading to America searching for a better life with no idea what awaited them upon arrival. We had heard stories of the sacrifices that had taken place in order for them to make this journey and we gave thanks as we ate our meal for the life that lay ahead of us.

When supper concluded at 7:30 pm we rose to leave the saloon. I thanked the stewards who were quick to clear the tables of our dishes. They returned a quick smile before hurrying off. James mentioned that he had spotted a friend earlier and was meeting him to play cards in the smoke room. Helen and I decided to return to our cabin and meet our roommates. Upon entry we found two women sitting on the lower bunk looking through letters.

"Hello, I'm Margaret and this is my sister-in-law, Mary," said the more slender of the two.

She had jet black hair held in a bun with two metal clips. Her eyes were a deep cobalt blue that expressed a touch of sadness. I extended my hand in welcome and introduced Helen and myself. Mary gave a slight smile as she took my hand in a delicate handshake, then quickly looked away. They were both from Ireland, near Dublin, yet Mary had lived in Chicago for quite some time. Her husband Joseph, Margaret's brother, worked there as an architect and was heavily involved in a project to develop the city along with American architect and urban developer, Daniel Burnham. He felt Chicago was on the verge of becoming a prominent city in America and had asked his sister to join him since their parents had recently passed away.

We talked for nearly half an hour before I excused myself. It was nearing sunset and I wanted to capture the image in my mind from the outside deck. I have always loved watching the sun set, and over the sea the sight was especially delightful. After putting on another layer of clothing to stay warm I headed back up to the promenade. As I stood watching the beautiful orange ball plummet into the sea, I thought of the land I had left behind. I thought of my family and my siblings, some so young I felt I did not know them. I thought about the life they would lead as I got on with my newfound one in America. Little did any of us know what the days ahead would bring?

CHAPTER 3

Day two aboard the *Titanic* began with a continuation of the sounds that had echoed throughout the night in our cabin, namely those of the engines in operation which caused a constant vibration that filled the room. Helen and I rose at 7:00 am eager to get on with our day at sea. After spending about an hour chatting with Margaret and Mary about life in general and our respective families, we took turns using the water basin to freshen up before dressing. All of us then headed up to the dining saloon on F-Deck for breakfast which began at 8:30 am. Once again there were two sittings, this time each lasting an hour. We chose the first and were met by James upon entry.

We made our way to a table and were greeted by the couple with their four children whom we had met yesterday. The boys were filled with energy once again and the father had to repeat his instruction to sit down more than once. The tables were set and the stewards began placing selections in front of us. Breakfast consisted of oatmeal porridge and milk, smoked herring with jacket potatoes, as well as tripe and onions. Fresh bread with butter and marmalade was served along with tea and coffee.

As we enjoyed our meal we talked with the family and learned more about their desires for the future upon their arrival in America. They envisioned traveling by train to nearby Pennsylvania in hopes of finding a small house with some farmland where the boys could have space to run and play. Just then I felt a tug at my dress and looked down. It was the youngest boy who had been sitting next to me.

"Did you see the magic man?" he asked.

"Magic man?" I replied.

"Yes, I saw him last night in the stairway. He showed me a trick and then he disappeared."

He then tried to wink but both his eyes closed and opened instead of just one. We all laughed out loud at his antics.

"Shhh," he responded and I politely nodded in agreement.

It was our secret. I smiled to myself and thought, "Who was this magic man?" I wondered what other secrets this ship held that I would discover during our voyage.

Following breakfast we said our farewells to the family and expressed our hopes of seeing them again. Helen and James decided to head out for another stroll about the ship. I returned briefly to our cabin to retrieve my book and then headed up to the Promenade on C-Deck. It was another beautiful day and the sky was so blue it reminded me of the sailor's eyes I had connected with when first arriving on board. I wondered what it was like to work aboard a ship as large as this one. There were so many stewards and others scurrying about.

When I reached the outside deck I found a long deck chair and sat down. I was anxious to return to my book as my curiosity had been piqued from where I left off yesterday. As I read I would pause every now and then and glance upwards as others walked by. I'd admire the couples and think of my beloved Robert. I'd smile at the children who seemed filled with innocence and joy. After about an hour I began to catch a chill. I was just about to get up when I heard a voice speak from behind me.

"Afternoon Miss!" I looked up to see the sailor I had encountered yesterday. "It's getting chilly. Perhaps you would be more comfortable inside?"

I smiled in agreement, but then told him how I loved hearing the sound of the waves and wish I could stay on the deck.

"Perhaps I could bring you a blanket so that you would be more comfortable," he replied.

"Could you? I would really appreciate that."

He held up one finger and stated he would quickly return.

Before long he was back with a blanket. He placed it on top of me and instantly I felt better.

"May I join you?" he asked.

I nodded yes and he pulled up another chair and then introduced himself as George.

I met his hand in greeting and replied, "My name is Bridget."

He informed me that he worked on the ship as part of the engineering crew, yet had several responsibilities for the duration of the voyage. He wasn't wearing his sailor's attire today and his shirt appeared to be a little big for his thin frame. He stood about six feet, perhaps a little taller. His dark hair allowed his eyes to be highlighted and their piercing blue color matched the sky's hue.

Listening to him tell his story was fascinating. He

came from Southampton, England, and prior to this voyage he had sailed with the *Titanic's* sister ship, the *Olympic*.

"What are you reading?" he asked.

I held up my book for him to see the cover. "*The Story Girl* by L.M. Montgomery.

Have you heard of the author?"

Lowering his head he replied, "I can't say that I have."

After looking over the book he handed it back to me and glanced around quickly.

"Well, I should go. It was nice meeting you."

Just then the young son of the couple from breakfast appeared and jumped up on my lap.

"OH!" I exclaimed.

He smiled and whispered in my ear. "I see you met the magic man."

When I looked around, George had disappeared.

"But... where did he go? He was just here."

The boy just smiled, gave me his two eye wink, and ran off.

The visit had distracted me from my reading and

now all of the sudden my curiosity was aroused even more, but this time about the supposed magic man. Who was he really? I folded up the blanket, placed it on the chair, and went back to the General Room in hopes of finding Helen and James. After a short time they emerged from the outside deck.

"How's your book?" Helen asked.

"What?" I replied faintly, feeling totally distracted.

"Your book. Didn't you go up to the Promenade to read?"

"Oh yes, sorry. I just had the most bizarre encounter with a slightly charming sailor."

Helen drew closer and with wide eyes replied, "Oh really?"

I didn't know exactly how to describe the encounter, so I just shook off the questions and suggested we go to dinner. I was getting hungry and eager to catch the early sitting at 1:00 pm.

As we entered the saloon I spotted Margaret and Mary and motioned for them to sit with us. We had another lovely meal and once again discussed their expectations for the voyage and the life they hoped to create in Chicago. I found it fascinating connecting with the other passengers and learning where they came from and where they were heading. America was such a large country with so much opportunity. Mr. William Taft was the President and Mr. James Sherman, a Republican from New York served under him as Vice President. I enjoyed learning about the country I had called home for the last five years, although my heart would always belong to my mother Ireland.

Following dinner, James decided to head to the Smoke Room to join his new friends for a game of cards. Helen and I decided to stroll around the ship and see what else we could discover. Margaret and Mary joined us. Next to our dining saloon on F-Deck there was housed a Swimming Bath as well as the luxurious Turkish Baths reserved for those in First Class. We weren't able to view them, but heard from one of the stewards that they were quite the spectacle. First Class passengers paid four shillings to experience the suite which consisted of a steam room, a hot room, a temperate room and a shampooing room. Those who visited would be able to get massages and take a dip in the adjacent salt water pool. At the conclusion of their sessions, guests could then relax in an area known as the Cooling Room.

The one area of the ship that I was really hoping to see was the Second Class Library that was housed far aft on the C-Deck next to our Promenade. I had passed it the first day and wanted so much to go in, but there were strict rules about the classes not mixing and each had their own special areas. On this day, however, we were able to converse with one of the stewards on the promenade who shared a little about the Library. Apparently it was decorated in Colonial Adams style, and was the only room on board to use an American style of décor.

As the steward informed us of the Library, how it was furnished and was occupied by the Second Class passengers, I envisioned what it must be like to experience such a room. I knew I would probably get lost in my books if allowed in there and would never again venture out on the decks no matter how much I loved the sound of the sea. I was about halfway through reading *The Story Girl* and hoped to complete it by the time we reached New York.

Following our tour of the ship we had built up quite an appetite and decided to take in the Afternoon Tea which was being offered. In addition to tea, we found a nice selection of food items consisting of pickled cod, curry and rice, as well as Swedish bread with butter and jam. James did not join us as he must have been winning at the card games, and remained in the Smoke Room. We enjoyed our tea, met more passengers, and had some great conversations.

After tea we decided to head back to the General Room which was next door to the Smoking Room. We figured that would be the first place James would look for us following the end of his card game, and where we had decided to meet prior to supper. It was during this time that I decided to share with Helen what had distracted me earlier in the day, namely the visit with George.

"So he just disappeared?" she asked.

"Yes, it was strange. We were having a lovely conversation and then all of the sudden he said he had to leave."

Helen raised an eyebrow and murmured, "Interesting."

I didn't want to make too much of the incident since I was looking to get married soon and probably shouldn't be having conversations with other men during this voyage. Yet, George seemed friendly enough and I didn't really feel our short conversation would hurt anyone.

As the playing of the bugle announced supper time, the corridors filled up with people coming from every direction. James entered the General Room and found us talking with some other guests.

"Ladies, shall we?" he asked motioning with his right hand towards the door.

We headed down the three levels to our dining saloon where we found the family of six entering as we approached. The youngest son ran up to me and tugged on my dress.

"Did you see the magic man again?" he whispered.

"Shhh," I replied. "Let's keep the magic man a secret between ourselves, shall we?"

He smiled in agreement.

"Charlie! Stopped bothering Miss Bridget!"

We both looked over and saw the child's mother waving her finger in the air. I smiled and assured her he was no bother.

Once again we enjoyed a fine supper and conversed with James to learn of his card games and the new friends he had made so far during the voyage.

"We had a fine time and I even won a few games. Some wise yoke from the crew came away the big winner and we wondered if he had some tricks up his sleeve."

I smiled and wondered if it were our magic man friend, George, and if I'd see him again.

Following our meal we headed back to the General Room for about an hour before retreating to our berths. I once again put on an extra layer of clothing so that I could view the sunset which commenced around half past eight. Helen remained in the cabin speaking with Margaret and Mary while I headed up to the Shelter Deck. The sky was a beautiful shade of pinks and orange hues and I was mesmerized by its beauty.

"Another evening masterpiece in the works, eh?"

I turned to find George standing in the doorway.

"Yes, it's so beautiful."

He approached and stood near me.

"Are you enjoying the voyage thus far?" he asked.

I smiled and nodded my head yes.

"These are my favorite moments: the stillness, the beauty, nature's bounty."

He smiled and returned a nod in agreement, then retreated just as quickly as he had arrived.

My curiosity continued to grow with every encounter with this mysterious man. Who was he really, and how did he seem to vanish so quickly as if he were inherent to the ship itself? A part of me felt it was inappropriate to have such curiosity about this man, yet I couldn't help it. Perhaps it was simply my curious nature getting the best of me, or the plots from all the books I'd lost myself in reading now playing with my mind. Returning to my cabin I dared not mention this encounter to Helen or she might begin to worry about me. Besides, I was tired and I just wanted to turn in early.

CHAPTER 4

Saturday welcomed our third day at sea and I grew more and more excited about what lie ahead in New York. Rising briskly at 7:00 am I decided to take a morning stroll to clear my head the memory of my encounter with George last night. Helen and the others were still sleeping when I exited the cabin and I quietly closed the door behind me as to not wake them. The ship was already a buzz with stewards and crew walking about preparing for another day at sea. I found my way through the corridors and stairways up to the Shelter Deck. I briefly stepped out onto the Promenade to welcome the day, but it was quite cold so I didn't spend much time there.

Just as I was about to head indoors, I heard a voice from behind.

"Miss Bridget!" I turned to find George hurrying up to me.

"You must have left this behind yesterday?" he continued as he held up my book.

"Oh my goodness. I hadn't even realized. Thank

you so much for returning it to me."

He smiled and motioned towards the door. "It is a bit chilly out this morning. Would you accompany me to the General Room?"

I nodded yes and proceeded to join him. When we arrived the room was fairly empty so we found a place to sit and converse. I was curious to learn more about this man.

As we passed by the Library I mentioned to him how fascinated I was with the room and had envisioned what it must be like to spend time there during the voyage. I told him about the stroll Helen and I had taken yesterday and all we had learned from the stewards we came across.

"Yes, she is quite the vessel. There are so many compartments that not even I know about all of them, but I'd love to show you some of my favorite spots if you'd like."

I smiled and thought it would be fun to explore the great ship, yet part of me hesitated in responding to his request.

"I don't know if I should," I replied.

"Oh come on. We'll even visit the forbidden spots."

He winked and held out his hand.

As we left the General Room and headed towards the stairwells, he looked around and motioned for me to follow him.

"We just need to make one quick stop first."

I followed him to the Upper Deck to Scotland Road where we then headed towards the Bow. Just as we were approaching the areas reserved for the Seaman's Quarters, he opened a side door and escorted me inside. It was a small room filled with supplies for the ship. As he went towards the back of the room I looked around, nervous someone would see us. He reappeared holding a man's jacket, tie and hat, along with a lady's hat and shawl.

"Here, put this on," he said handing me the hat and shawl.

He then put on the jacket, tie and hat and smiled.

"This will help us get to where we need to go," he said while also applying a pair of spectacles.

My eyes grew wide with both excitement and fear, yet I was a spontaneous person, so why not play along?

After applying our disguises, he opened the door and peeked out, looking in both directions.

"Let's go!" he instructed, and off he ran with me following him up the stairwell to the Saloon Deck.

"We're going all the way up, so just stay behind me."

I followed in silence and did as he instructed. We reached the Shelter Deck and then he motioned me towards another stairwell. We continued going up stairs until we reached the Bridge Deck.

"Okay, now take my arm and just act as if you belong here."

I followed along as we walked down the corridor which housed the Millionaire's suites. It was still fairly early and preparations were being made to welcome the new day. The Bridge Deck housed the Restaurant Reception Room along with the First Class Restaurant and Café Parisien. It also accommodated the Second Class Smoke Room.

We entered the area housed by the Café and I was mesmerized. It was everything I had envisioned a Paris street café to be. Decorated with French trellis work with ivy and large picture windows, it was beautiful.

"WOW! This is magnificent," I exclaimed.

George smiled and then held out his hand.

"Come, I want to show you something even more

magnificent."

He led me through the reception area to the Grand Staircase. It was the most beautiful sight I had ever witnessed. I had heard about the grand staircase, but never envisioned actually seeing it in person. It rose beautifully and spanned six decks. Decorated with oak panels and gilded balustrades, I was left speechless and in awe of its magnificence.

As I stood there gazing at this incredible piece of architecture, the sounds of people moving about startled me. George took my hand and motioned for us to head down the staircase. We found ourselves on the Shelter Deck near the Maid's and Valet's Saloon. We continued down the corridor towards the bow end of the ship where we approached the forward staircase.

"Come! This leads us back down to Scotland Road."

I followed George down each level, quickly glancing about to capture an image in my mind's eye. When we reached the Upper Deck he asked for the hat and shawl. I obliged, passing them to him and watching his face as it lit up with a big smile.

"Until next time," he said as he scurried off.

As I turned to head back to my cabin I passed a steward.

"Could you tell me the time sir?" I asked.

"It's half past nine Miss."

I thanked him and then scurried off myself. It was already time for the second breakfast sitting and Helen and the others would be concerned as to where I was on the ship. I entered the dining saloon and found them waiting at one of the tables.

"Bridget! Where have you been? We saved you a seat."

I smiled at Helen and sat down.

"So sorry everyone. I wanted to go for a walk this morning around the ship and simply lost track of time."

As I spread butter and marmalade onto a fresh biscuit I couldn't help but think of everything I had just experienced. I had spent the last two hours with a man I hardly knew on an adventure I could have only dreamt of. I thought of all the things I had seen and what it must be like to live in such luxury. I was content with my life and excited about my future with Robert, yet this was something new; a lifestyle I didn't feel I'd ever get a glimpse of seeing. As Helen and the others talked amongst themselves I was left in my own little world curious as to what would happen next.

Following breakfast Helen mentioned she was meeting up with Margaret and Mary to take a stroll around the ship. After the adventure I had just been on I suggested she'd go without me as I wanted to get back to reading my book. I decided to do so in my cabin and that is where I retreated to following our meal. As I opened my book I thought of George and how sweet it was of him to retrieve my lost item and find me to return it. I thought of our morning adventure and all we had seen together. My mind floated back and forth between the story on the pages and the one in my memory. I hadn't anticipated such an experience during this journey.

Nearly three hours had passed when I opened my eyes. Apparently I had fallen asleep while reading and it was nearing time for dinner. Helen suggested we'd meet for the second sitting at 1:45 pm so they would have more time to explore the ship. I agreed. I headed up to the Saloon and met her and the others there where we enjoyed another excellent meal and conversation. As we were leaving the Saloon young Charlie approached and tugged on my skirt.

"Have you seen the magic man, Miss?" he asked with a big smile across his face.

"I have!" I replied. "He showed me some of his tricks," I replied while winking at him.

His eyes widened as he put his hand to his mouth to cover the sound of giggles and scurried away.

Watching young Charlie run off made me laugh as I marveled at his innocence and curiosity when it came to George. What he must think of the sailor and his tricks. George had a delightful personality so it was easy to like him. He was very charming and could easily make me laugh with his clever jargon. He appeared very knowledgeable about all aspects of the ship, and yet I didn't really know much about his duties onboard. He briefly mentioned working with the engineers, yet also seemed very at home when we were visiting the First Class lounges. He had certainly piqued my curiosity, and I simply enjoyed his company.

The afternoon was fairly lazy as Helen and I decided to retreat to the Promenade and chat about our lives and dreams, what lie ahead in New York, and what we were leaving behind in Ireland. Having lived in America for nearly five years I had a pretty good idea of what Helen would enjoy and what she would find different from our native Ireland. I shared with her my favorite parts of New York, especially the new main branch of the public library that had opened on Fifth Avenue last year. The structure was magnificent and was said to have housed over one million books.

There had been a dedication ceremony and even President Taft had attended.

As supper time approached and the temperatures on deck began to fall, we moved into the General Room where we found a few of the passengers playing instruments and couples dancing. We sat and watched for a while until James arrived and asked Helen to dance. I decided to sit this one out when he asked me for the next dance. I was more comfortable simply observing. At 6:45 pm we headed to the Saloon for supper. We found young Charlie and his family there as well and enjoyed a lovely conversation. Following dinner we retreated to our cabin.

Once again I wanted to experience the sunset. I asked Helen if she'd like to come with me this time, but she declined saying she didn't desire to be outdoors in the cold. I put on the extra layer of clothing to stay warm and headed back up to the Promenade. As I was approaching the outside deck, George quickly appeared.

"Miss Bridget! Would you care to join me for another adventure tomorrow morning?"

I smiled and nodded yes in agreement.

"Half past seven I shall meet you in the General Room," he stated as he hurried off.

I smiled thinking of what new things we would see and experience.

After viewing another beautiful sunset I retreated to my berth in hopes of re-reading the passages of my book I had attempted to read earlier in the day. I found Helen writing in her journal and Margaret and Mary speaking quietly with each other. The time had passed quickly these three days and we were now approaching the halfway mark of our voyage. Soon we would be in New York and my new life as Robert's wife would begin. I closed my book and my eyes in hopes of drifting off into a dream-filled sleep.

Sunday morning I woke earlier than anticipated, around 6:00 am. I lay in bed thinking about George and what this day would bring, wondering what adventure was in store. Finally at 7:00 am I rose and prepared for the day. I quietly left the cabin and headed up to the Shelter Deck to meet George in the General Room. He appeared at 7:30 am sharp and directed me to follow him back to the room we had visited the day before that housed the ship's supplies. Once again dressed in our upscale disguises, he led me up the stairwells, this time to A-Deck, the Promenade level which housed numerous rooms designated for First Class passengers only.

Heading towards the Stern side of the ship from

the formal staircase we snuck a peek at the Reading and Writing Room which was a place many of the ladies frequented. The room had white walls with tall windows complete with pink curtains, and was warmed by a coal burning fireplace. Tall potted ferns were placed throughout the room to add extra coziness to it. George mentioned they had a library where one could check out books and the tables were used to write letters and post them. It was a beautiful room and even more stunning than that of the Second Class Library.

Next to the Reading and Writing Room we found the First Class Lounge which was unlike anything I had ever seen. It was a massive room with twelve foot ceilings with oak paneling on the walls. It housed tables, chairs, sofas and lounges upholstered in velvet, all decorated with green and gold floral patterns. According to George it was modeled in the style of Louis XV after the Palace of Versailles in Paris. It was breathtaking. Next to the seating area were small alcoves with tall bay windows and stained glass panes at the top. The vibrant colors glistened with the sun's light beaming in from the sea.

We then continued on our adventure passing by the Smoke Room to the rear of the ship where we found both the Verandah and Palm Court, two rooms each one half of the ship in size with a shared pantry and a Smoke Room which allowed for light refreshments. According to George, the port side café was the room mainly used as the smoking section since it had revolving doors to the Smoke Room. The starboard side, which sat empty most of the time was used as a play room for the children of the First Class passengers.

As we were making our way back towards the Bow of the ship, George accidently bumped into another gentleman walking by us. Puzzled, the man gave George a stern look, and then one of perhaps familiarity. George quickly took my arm and ushered me down the corridor.

"I may have been discovered. We should go!" he exclaimed.

We hurried towards the staircase, made our way down to the Bridge Deck, then to the Shelter Deck, finally reaching the Saloon Deck where he asked for the items he had lent me.

"Until next time, my fair lady," he said with a smile as he kissed my hand.

I returned his smile and before I knew it, he was gone.

CHAPTER 5

Lily

Coronado, California
April, 2012

Bright sunshine greeted me after my first full night's sleep in Coronado. After spending the last forty-eight hours putting furniture together, unpacking boxes, and setting up utilities, I finally woke in my own bed in my new island home. I had put together a massive To Do list and was anxious to get started on it. I figured I'd give myself a week to get settled, explore my new surroundings, and then get back to work. Today was all about making connections. First stop, the Chamber of Commerce. I introduced myself and mentioned I had just moved into the area. I was provided with a Visitor's Guide and a few pieces of literature for new residents. I checked out the post office, the grocery store, and the best ways to see the island. I didn't have a car, but I enjoyed walking and riding my bike. It was such a beautiful day I decided to take the ferry across to San Diego and purchased a

Compass Card at the MTS store. That way I could ride public transportation by simply adding money to it whenever I needed to travel.

Everywhere I went I was greeted by the locals with a hearty hello and either a nod of their head or slight wave. I loved that I could easily walk everywhere I needed to go within a half hour. From my new home to the ocean was twenty-five minutes and five to fifteen minutes to San Diego Bay and Glorietta Bay respectfully. I loved exploring and felt very much at home here. It was a new city, but had such a warm community feel, that made me feel comfortable as soon as I arrived. I passed by the local hardware store and spotted some beautiful colored Adirondack chairs. I thought they would be perfect for my large deck at home, so I ordered five of them in multiple colors. The owner said he'd be happy to deliver them since I lived just a couple blocks away.

In the afternoon I headed out to explore the Hotel del Coronado, or the Del as the famous hotel has come to be known by the locals. I had visited it before, but now knowing it was practically in my backyard and I could visit as often as I'd like was a thrill. After walking the grounds I headed out to the beach where I found a man creating a magnificent sandcastle. I learned his name was Bill and he was actually known as "The Sandcastle Man." We chatted for a while as I admired his work. Whatever name he went by, he was very talented. I then decided to head to the Community Center where I learned of the different facilities and activities available, and special rates for locals. The Aquatics Center was impressive and I looked forward to spending time there.

After leaving the Community Center, I headed across the street to check out the beach area south of the Del in front of the Shores condominiums. While chatting with some of the locals I heard about the buzz going on around town. Apparently a shipwreck had resurfaced on the beach near the Shores and nearly half a million dollars in silver coins had been discovered in the last week. I was curious to learn more and see if I could spot the vessel. When I arrived on the beach there were signs posted in the sand warning of the dangers of an underwater obstruction, but I couldn't see anything. Apparently it was only visible when the low tide reached negative digits.

On the way home I strolled down Orange Avenue, stopping in shops and picking up small pieces of decor for my new home. I was a beach girl, a mermaid really, and I wanted my home to reflect my free spirit with a nautical theme throughout. I picked up a collection of seashells and other pieces I admired, and once I returned home I pulled out my To Do list and began crossing off things I had accomplished. I was settling in quite nicely and felt good about my decision to move. It was strange, but in a way I felt like I had been here before, and not just as a visitor. There was a familiarity in the air, a sense of peace that I hadn't felt in a long time.

As evening approached I wrote in my journal about my day and all I had seen and accomplished, the people I had met, and everything I had learned about my new community. I thought of Santa Monica and how much I had loved living there. Even though there were moments when I missed being there, somehow I knew I was precisely where I was supposed to be. Just then my cell phone rang.

"Hey Lil! It's Kate!" said the voice on the other end.

"Oh hey, Kate. How goes it?"

It was nice to hear from my friend. She was just checking in to see how I was doing and I filled her in on what I had been up to since arriving, and all I had learned.

The great part about the last few days was the dream hadn't visited me during the night, and I'd had no visions or murmurs. I was certainly happy about that. I suppose it's because my mind had been so occupied on the move that there was no room for anything else at that time. I knew however, that the time would come where I needed to face the dream and get answers to the questions I had about it. At least I felt comfortable enough here to begin exploring the meaning behind the dream.

After a couple more days of familiarizing myself with the town and some days of much needed rest, I was ready to get back to work. I decided to kick off the week by stopping by the newspaper office first thing the next morning. The local *Gazette* was a short fifteen minute walk from my new home and it was yet another gorgeous day in paradise. As I entered the small office I was greeted by a cheerful receptionist.

"Is Tom Jeffrey's available?" I asked.

Responding with a big smile, she answered, "Oh! You mean TJ?"

I smiled slightly, nodded yes, and was asked to have a seat.

A moment later TJ, as his friends and colleagues knew him, appeared at the door.

"Lily! So great to see you. Welcome to Nado!"

I thanked him and we went into another room. I

noticed a few others scurrying about and asked if it were a bad time to talk with him.

"Never a bad time for you Lil, but we are getting ready to cover an event in the city. Perhaps you could join us. Hold on a sec."

He then left the office and I could hear him talking with another man. He returned with a big grin on his face.

"You have your camera, I imagine?" he asked.

I nodded yes.

"Perfect! You're IN!"

He motioned towards the door and we headed out.

As we approached a white van, TJ introduced me to the man I heard him talking to earlier.

"This is Jason Ridgeley, one of our writers."

I shook hands with him.

"Thanks for helping us out, kid! We're a small outfit and can always use an extra hand."

I smiled, happy to help, yet I had no idea where we were heading. As we crossed the Coronado/San Diego Bridge, I asked,

"Where are we going and what is the assignment?

TJ answered with another big grin on his face.

"This is a big one, huge event. We're on our way to the Natural History Museum for their *Titanic* Centennial festivities. It's a week-long event and the action kicks off today."

San Diego's Natural History Museum is located in Balboa Park which is this massive piece of architectural genius. It was a short fifteen minute drive from the island. We parked in a nearby lot and everyone gathered their equipment. The museum was hosting an exhibit entitled, *Titanic*: *The Artifact Exhibition* with tickets specially priced at $19.12 during the week to reflect the hundred year anniversary. In addition to the exhibit, guests would enjoy live demonstrations of replica radios used on the *Titanic*, interactions with actors sharing passenger stories, as well as different *Titanic* themed movies being shown throughout the week. There was also a very special dinner at the nearby Prado restaurant that would replicate the First-Class dining experience aboard the ship.

Upon entering the museum we were greeted by the exhibit's media person who was part of the company, Premiere Exhibitions which organized the exhibit tour across the country. They'd also brought along their own spokesperson, an actor dressed as Captain Smith from the *Titanic*, in full costume. We were led up to the second floor where over eight hundred square feet of space had been set aside to host the exhibit. Jason and TJ scoped out the area and discussed how best to cover the story. TJ motioned for me to join them.

"Hey Lil. We're going to interview some of the actors portraying the passengers and also some of the staff. Why don't you try to capture some stills of the exhibit and interaction between guests and the actors?"

I happily agreed and set off to see what interesting shots I could capture.

The exhibit provided quite the experience as the first thing guests received upon entering was their own boarding pass from White Star Line. On the back they found the name of a passenger from the ship along with details including where they were from, age and who they were accompanied by during the voyage. Below that they found their class, where they were traveling to and the reason behind being aboard. There was also a space marked, *Passenger Fact:* which gave a little personal information about the passenger.

Actors from the American Rose Theatre portrayed passengers and crew members from the *Titanic,* and were dressed as characters from the 1912 era in full costume depicting the period. They talked with guests about life aboard the great ship and personal details about the actual passengers, each with their own intriguing story. I captured some shots of this interaction and couldn't help but overhear the stories they shared. I found it fascinating. I knew the general story of the *Titanic* as it was highly publicized and took on a life of its own again in 1997 with the release of James Cameron's film of the same name, but this was more of a hands on experience.

The exhibit was quite spectacular as it housed an impressive collection of artifacts retrieved from the ship when the wreck was explored in the late 1980s. Several of the main areas had also been reconstructed such as the Grand Staircase and the accommodations for both First and Third Class passengers, yet the exhibit varied city by city depending on the available space at each destination. I also captured photos of these areas. There was also an area where volunteers from the USS Midway Museum reenacted radio demonstrations to show how the distress calls had taken place from the *Titanic*. Throughout the weekend, these same amateur radio operators would be using modern equipment to communicate with a ship positioned over the *Titanic's* wreck site in the North Atlantic. Those who would be aboard that ship would be communicating with other amateur radio operators worldwide.

As I was capturing photos I had the opportunity to stop and chat with some of the actors portraying passengers. Their stories were fascinating, and I also learned more about what they had scheduled for the week. The dinner at Prado sounded amazing and I would love to attend, yet $212 a ticket was a little out of my price range. I knew I needed to budget wisely since I had just moved. My mind raced with excitement however when I learned of what was planned. It was a ten-course meal replicating the final dinner served on the *Titanic* for the First-Class passengers of the ship, and included five expertly paired wines. Guests would be served in Prado's Grand Ballroom by a staff wearing white period tuxedo jackets. There was also a piano quintet playing tunes specifically from 1912. Tickets were limited to one hundred guests and I could only image what a spectacular experience it would be.

The museum was extending its hours throughout the week specifically for the Centennial celebration, and on Saturday, the night of the dinner, it would remain open until 3:00 am to accommodate those who wished to visit the exhibit following dinner. The dinner ticket also included entry to the exhibit. After about an hour shooting photos and chatting with both staff and guests, I met back up with TJ and Jason. As we were about to exit the museum, we were stopped by

Premiere's media liaison person who handed each of us an exhibit ticket and invited us to return. I was grateful as I wanted to visit again when I had more time.

We boarded the van and headed back across the bridge to Coronado to the newspaper office. Once there Jason thanked me for helping out and TJ asked when I could have the photos to him.

"I can head home and edit them now, and get them to you in a couple hours," I responded.

"Perfect!" he replied.

Once home I uploaded the photos from my camera to my laptop and began the editing process. As I was sorting through them, a couple caught my eye, and triggered a visual flash in my mind. There was one I had captured of the Third Class accommodations which was made up of a pair of bunk beds with a water basin between them. It seemed so familiar, yet I couldn't figure out how or why. Another photo that caused feelings of déjà vu was a shot of the lifeboats. With that one, it was more of a feeling of familiarity instead of a memory. I just shook them off and continued working, eventually uploading the new files to a Dropbox and emailed the link to TJ.

A couple hours later, the phone rang. It was TJ.

"Hey Lil. These photos are great. Boss man loves them and asked about you. He wants to know if you'd like to help us out again, sort of a freelance gig."

"Wow," I thought. That would be great as I'd been hoping to work there.

"Yes! I'd love to." I replied.

"Great! We'll stay in touch."

I hung up the phone and was thrilled for the news. That didn't take long, I thought. Things were beginning to take shape in my new environment.

CHAPTER 6

Coronado, California
April, 2012

The following morning I decided I didn't want to wait to return to the *Titanic* exhibit later in the week. I would go back today. I couldn't escape the feelings I had when I looked at the photos and curiosity had gotten the best of me. I used my Compass Card to take the bus over to San Diego. The trip wasn't bad as I only had to take two buses and the trip took about forty-five minutes. It was a nice day and I didn't have any place else to be, so I didn't mind the trip. The bus stop I chose was across the street from the Natural History Museum. As I entered and handed over my ticket, I was greeted by Captain Smith, or should I say Lowell Lytle, the actor portraying the famed Captain of the *Titanic*.

We had a chance to chat for a bit and he said I looked familiar. I mentioned visiting yesterday with the newspaper and he smiled as he remembered. I was given a boarding pass from White Star Line and this one had the name Dr. Alice Leader (Alice Farnham) listed as the passenger name. According to the pass, she was forty-nine years old from New York and traveling in First Class from Southampton, England back to New York, US. She had been accompanied by her friend, Frederick J. Swift. The reason given for her trip mentioned that she had retired from her medical practice in Lewiston, Maine after the death of her husband in 1908, and was returning from a holiday in Europe. It was stated that although she practiced pediatric medicine, she had no children.

The exhibit was truly magnificent and contained over two hundred pieces of artifacts recovered from the wreck, some of which had never been displayed on the West Coast. There were dishes and menus, shoes and perfume bottles, jewelry and books. I was amazed at how some of the pieces had remained in such great condition considering the journey they took to the bottom of the sea and throughout the recovery. There were also areas reconstructed to resemble both the First and Third Class accommodations. Although the First Class rooms were stunning and impressive, they didn't evoke the emotion I felt as much as those from Third Class. Once again viewing the room with the bunk beds, I felt as if somehow I knew that room.

The same feeling ensued when I explored the

photographs of the different classes, and also those of the crew members. There was also an area that was decorated to resemble Café Parisien with its checkered floor and French décor. One room contained a large replica of an iceberg that was even cool to the touch. Actors dressed in Edwardian-era costumes walked through the exhibit sharing stories of the passengers and crew, and the actor dressed as Captain Smith even recited some of the final speech the Captain had delivered prior to going down with his ship. It was quite moving.

As I entered every room I took time to really visit each artifact that was showcased, whether on its own, or part of a glass case that contained an assortment of items. I couldn't help but notice my emotions as I looked at certain pieces, once again causing a familiarity I couldn't explain. I began to think about my dream and piece together what I had remembered and what I was feeling as I explored the exhibit. I looked down at my Boarding Pass but didn't feel any type of connection to this doctor whose name appeared. I thought perhaps it was just all in my head and I was looking for answers where none were to be found.

As the tour concluded I approached a large wall that contained a list of the names of those who survived the disaster. They were organized by class and crew. As I skimmed through the names, two jumped out at me. One was a Third Class passenger named Bridget.

"Bridget Rose" I whispered to myself, as if saying the name would trigger a memory. It didn't.

Yet there was something about her name that triggered emotions I didn't quite know what to make of. The other name was that of a crew member, George William. I felt the same emotions, as if there were a connection between the two, yet couldn't put my finger on what it was. I shook it off and exited the exhibit.

Instead of immediately heading home, I decided to spend the rest of the afternoon walking around Balboa Park, taking in the different museums and strolling through the parklands. I reflected on what I had experienced while walking through the exhibit and thought about my dream. Was there some type of connection between the two or was I simply grasping at straws?

I took the bus back towards the bay and decided to visit Seaport Village and take in the sights. I was impressed by the beauty of the bay as well as the shops and attractions that filled the space. I loved being so close to the water. Somehow it felt like home.

It was such a beautiful day that I decided to take the ferry home. I purchased a ticket through the Flagship Cruises ticket office and boarded the boat at the Broadway Street ramp. As I was walking down the ramp I heard someone call from behind me.

"Bridget, wait for me!" echoed the voice.

I turned to find a young man waving his arm and looked around me to see who he was waving to. Suddenly I spotted a young girl with dark auburn hair and fair skin waving back. The young man hurried down the ramp past me, met the girl with a warm embrace and then they boarded the ferry together. I thought of the name I had seen on the wall at the exhibit, Bridget Rose, and what the significance could mean.

The ferry ride was lovely and only took fifteen minutes to cross San Diego Bay. I decided to capture some photos along the way, first of the San Diego skyline and then of the Coronado Bridge which was quite the sight with its blue curved design that seemed perfectly placed to connect the island to the mainland. Once we disembarked it was only a short five minute stroll home.

The afternoon was passing by and I was hungry. I decided to fix some lunch and sit out on my deck to eat and also write in my journal of my experience at the exhibit. I pulled some kale salad out of the fridge and chopped up fresh strawberries. I then fixed a plate of tuna and mixed it all together in a bowl, adding a touch of cheddar on top. I then took out the large pitcher of water with fresh lemon from the fridge and poured a glass. After placing my meal on a side table on the deck, I grabbed my journal and made myself comfortable in one of my Adirondack chairs which had been delivered the day before.

As I took a fork full of my salad I started writing in my journal. I wrote of everything I had experienced while exploring the exhibit and how the two names jumped out at me and how I was curious about their significance. I even mentioned the couple on the ferry and how hearing the name Bridget startled me a bit. Could it have just been a coincidence or something else? I wrote of connecting with TJ and how happy I was to see a friend and how I felt about calling the island home. This place made me feel comfortable even though I had only been here a short time.

I wrote about my life in Santa Monica and how I'd had so many big plans for my life there. Yet somehow I also felt as though I was precisely where I was supposed to be, here on Coronado. I briefly closed my eyes and thought of what new adventures I would encounter living here on the island and wondered where life would take me next.

CHAPTER 7

Bridget

RMS *Titanic*
April 14, 1912

As I made my way down the stairway from the Saloon Deck to the Upper Deck I learned it was only 9:00 am, so I had some time before the second breakfast sitting. I decided to return to my cabin and freshen up a bit before heading to our dining saloon. When I arrived there I found Margaret and Mary preparing for the day.

"Where's Helen?," I asked.

"Oh, she left with James about thirty minutes ago for a stroll about until breakfast," replied Margaret.

"She asked me to inform you that they will meet you in the Saloon if you returned."

I smiled and thanked her.

After washing my face with water from the basin and combing my hair, I headed off to the Saloon to join Helen and James for breakfast. We enjoyed a lovely meal and had a great conversation with some of the guests who were seated at our table. One was a young girl named Jane who was traveling to America with her parents in search of a better life. She was a bright girl from a small town near Dublin. She spoke of her dreams and what she envisioned her life to be like once arriving in New York. She also loved to read and we spoke of the books we had brought with us for the voyage. I shared with her *The Story Girl* and she was excited to read it and learn more about the *Anne of Green Gables* story. I knew she would enjoy it and said as much.

Following breakfast I wanted to venture out on the deck to read for a bit before the morning services, but the temperature had dropped significantly and the breeze was a little too strong to bear. We decided to just remain in the General Room until Father Byles was ready. Morning services were conducted on Sunday for each class and ours followed the Second Class. Robert had given me some beautiful tokens of his affections after we announced our engagement, and one was a beautiful cross on a chain which I wore around my neck. During the service I held onto it and thought of our reunion. I missed him so and anxiously awaited our arrival in New York.

After a lovely service, Helen and James decided to take a stroll around the ship and I decided to head back to our cabin and continue reading my book. I was so close to the end and was anxious to complete it. We then met up for the second dinner sitting in the Saloon which was very nice. Everyone was excited about having reached the midway point of our voyage and the anticipation of reaching America continued to grow. As usual, I overheard conversations of dreams shared and what lie ahead. Helen and I talked about my upcoming wedding which was scheduled for August. We wanted a summer wedding so that we could spend time outdoors with everything in bloom. I was so excited to begin this next chapter of my life, and in no time, our voyage would come to an end.

We spent the remainder of the afternoon in the General Room which was nearly filled to capacity as everyone had moved inside due to the cold temperature. Children were scattered about, playing on the floor or running around while the adults conversed amongst one another. It was a lovely afternoon. As the evening approached, a group of adults pulled out their instruments and began performing musical selections while others danced. James and Helen took to the dance floor as I watched.

"Pardon me Miss. May I have this dance?"

I turned around to find George with his hand extended towards me.

"George! What are you doing here?" I asked.

"I was just about to get some sleep before my next shift, but couldn't resist one more dance. Would you do me the honor?" he asked again with his hand still held out for mine.

I took his hand and we began to dance.

As he twirled me around and we laughed, I couldn't help but feel guilty thinking of Robert. During our conversations I hadn't mentioned I was engaged, only that I was meeting friends in New York.

"George, there's something I need to tell you," I said as he pulled me closer, looking at me intently with those sparkling blue eyes of his.

"Remember I said I was meeting up with friends when we reach New York? Well…"

"Shhh Miss," he whispered placing his right index finger across my lips.

"The night is passing us by. Let's just enjoy this moment."

He drew me closer and held me in his arms as the music slowed. I felt so comfortable with his strong arms around me, yet also felt nervous that Helen or

James would notice how close we were to one another.

"Dear Bridget. Would you be up for another adventure tonight, just a short stroll?"

"Oh, I don't know if I should. We're meeting some new friends for supper and then I really should retire for the evening."

"I know you'll enjoy the surprise I have," George continued. "Meet me at the supply room at 8:00pm. I promise I will have you back in no time."

"Alright. I shall meet you then."

I looked around to find Helen and James dancing. They appeared lost in their own world, laughing and singing along with the others as the musicians played.

"Until then, Miss Bridget," he said, releasing me from his grasp and then left the room.

Helen then approached me.

"Was that the sailor you mentioned?" she asked.

"Yes," I replied, not really sure what to make of the encounter.

"He's a bit of a mystery though, isn't he," she responded.

"He's handsome, but don't forget about that wonderful man you have waiting for you in New York."

The more I thought about George, the more curious I became about him and why we had connected. With two days remaining on board I was determined to learn more about him. What exactly did he do on this ship, and how did he go about nearly unnoticed? These were questions I needed answers to.

We gathered in the Saloon for supper at 6:45 pm and had a lovely meal. I was still pre-occupied with George and trying to figure out who he was. Perhaps I was just making too much of it. Possibly he was just a nice sailor who was lonely and seeking a companion to converse with on the voyage. I could only imagine what it must be like to work on a ship of this size and spend so much time at sea. He had mentioned that he had worked on the *Olympic* as well, so I imagined that it would get lonely after a while.

Following supper I returned to our cabin to find Margaret and Mary reading. Helen and James had decided to return to the General Room as they heard a party was taking place with music and dancing. Helen loved to dance so took advantage of every opportunity offered during the voyage to kick up her heels so to speak. I preferred relaxing and getting lost in one of my books. I had a little bit of time before I was to meet George, so I sat with Margaret and Mary and asked about their day. After a few minutes, I then excused myself mentioning I wanted to once again view the sunset. I retrieved my coat and left the cabin.

As I approached the supply room I found George waiting. We once again went inside and he put together another disguise for both of us. This time he wore a top hat and dark overcoat. He handed me a beautiful wool wrap that I placed over my coat.

"Perfect!" he exclaimed as he adjusted his hat.

"Where are we going?" I asked.

"Just wait and see. I know you'll love it."

I followed him up the staircase to D-Deck where we found the First Class Lounge which led into the First Class Dining Saloon.

"There's a big party tonight and I thought you'd enjoy it."

As I looked around the room I felt as though I had stepped into a dream. The men appeared quite dashing in their black suits and the women in beautiful gowns dripping with jewels. My eyes grew wide as they moved from person to person taking in their ensembles.

Then I saw it, the most beautiful piece of jewelry I had ever come across. It was a stunning blue heart-shaped stone surrounded in diamonds held by a simply silver chain that hung around the neck of an equally stunning woman.

"WOW! Look at that!" I whispered softly to George.

"Ah yes, the heart. It's beautiful isn't it? I heard it was an engagement present.

"It's so beautiful," I continued.

I stood in a state of awe as the stone glistened when the light caught its reflection. I couldn't take my eyes off of it. It was truly magnificent, and quite appropriate I thought to wear on an equally magnificent ship.

"Come, follow me," directed George.

I took his hand and we moved into the Saloon where an extravagant dinner was being served. The place cards on the table indicated it was a ten-course meal beginning with hors d'oeuvres and oysters.

"We shouldn't, George. Someone will take notice of us."

"Relax, my lady. We're just observing," he said with a wink of his eye.

As the passengers began filing into the Saloon for dinner, George motioned for me to follow. We retreated back into the reception area and down the stairway to the Upper Deck. When we reached Scotland Road, George asked for the wool wrap and hat I had been wearing as my disguise. He then took my hand and kissed it.

"Thank you for joining me this evening Miss Bridget. I had a lovely time."

I smiled, thanked him and retreated to my cabin. It was nearly 9:00 pm when I returned and found Margaret and Mary chatting. Helen had not yet returned. I read until approximately 10:00 pm and then prepared to turn in. Helen came back to the cabin shortly after stating the crew had turned out the lights in the General Room at 10:00 pm as well.

By 10:30 pm we were all in bed ready to sleep. Margaret and Mary fell asleep rather quickly followed by Helen. I lay in my berth thinking of all I had seen at the party and that magnificent stone necklace. I smiled thinking of George and all I had experienced since meeting the sailor. I was tired and looking forward to a good night's sleep. It wasn't difficult to sleep as we had become accustomed to the constant vibration made by the engines since our berths were so close to the boiler rooms. In a way it was a welcoming sound and feeling instead of silence and stillness. I occupied the top bunk which I liked because there was less of a disturbance when my bunk mate entered and exited the berth, as opposed to being on the bottom bunk. The rooms were tiny but had all the conveniences we required. Large public toilet rooms were also provided, yet only two bath tubs for those of us in steerage, one for the men and the other for the women. Plus I was more interested in what treasures were found around the rest of the ship, and felt lucky to have had seen so much up to that point, thanks to George. Before long, I fell into a dream state.

About an hour had passed when all of the sudden we felt a strong jolt, so strong it nearly knocked me from the berth. Mary who occupied the top bunk of the other bed was also startled and screamed in the confusion.

"What was that?" yelled Helen.

"I don't know," Margaret replied as she looked after Mary.

"Perhaps we just hit some ice?" I stated.

"I heard we were passing through some ice fields which would explain the temperature falling, but sure it's nothing serious. The *Titanic* is massive and I'm sure we're fine."

The truth was, I wasn't sure, and I felt something was seriously wrong.

Once I rose from the bed and comforted Mary, I rushed to the door to see what had happened. A steward passed by and said everything was okay and to just go back to sleep. Somehow I didn't feel reassured by his words and told Helen and the others we should remain in the cabin and await James as Helen was sure he would be arriving shortly as he must have felt the jolt as well. As we waited suddenly there was silence and a stillness we had not experienced throughout the journey. The repetitive vibration we had become so accustomed to, had simply stopped.

"Something is wrong and I don't have a good feeling about this," I said to the others.

It was quarter past midnight when James banged on the cabin door and I answered.

"Hurry!" he exclaimed.

"Put on your life belts and let's go."

We each did as he instructed.

"What's wrong? What happened?" I asked.

"Something is seriously wrong," he replied.

"I was thrown from my berth and there was

water coming into my cabin. We must have hit something big."

We each put on our coats and shoes and then placed our life belts on top of our clothing before heading out into the passageway. By this time the stewards began yelling "Everybody on deck with life belts on, at once!" Everyone was scurrying about and we didn't know which way to go.

We headed down the passageway to the stairwell that led up to the Middle Deck. However, when we reached that level, the gate was closed as it opened to the Second class rooms. We backtracked down again and then to another stairwell that led up. We managed to get up to the Upper Deck and followed Scotland Road towards another stairwell. People were running in every direction so we chose the closest stairwell. Once again we found a locked gate.

"This is crazy. Let's us in!" demanded James.

We continued to bang on the gate to no response. Suddenly we heard a loud bang.

"What's that?" yelled Margaret.

"Rockets!" replied James.

"We have to find a way out of here."

Once again we backtracked down and then

over to another stairwell. By this point droves of people had emerged and it was becoming more and more difficult to navigate where we were going. Many of those in our class did not speak English and couldn't understand the signage. We tried to guide as many as we could who appeared lost, but it just seemed futile.

Suddenly Margaret asked, "Where's Mary?"

We all looked around but she was nowhere to be found.

"Mary! Mary!" screamed Margaret.

"We have to find her."

In all the confusion she must have lost her way. We tried to retrace our steps, but had no luck in finding her.

James offered to stay behind with Margaret and search for Mary, and urged Helen and I to continue on trying to reach the Boat Deck.

"I'm not leaving you!" shouted Helen.

James turned to comfort her and assure her everything would be okay. As he held Helen in his arms, Margaret ran through the crowd.

"Margaret! Come back!" I yelled.

It was no use, she had disappeared into the

crowd.

"There's nothing more we can do here," exclaimed James.

Time was passing us by and we knew we needed to hurry. We finally reached the Shelter Deck that housed most of our class' accommodations and felt some relief.

That relief however, was quickly squashed. We reached the top of the stairwell only to find another locked gate because it led to the First Class Restaurant. Panic driven and exhausted, we decided to stop. We sat down in the stairwell and Helen began to weep. James held her and assured her everything would be okay. I pulled out my rosary and prayer book, two items I managed to grab from our cabin before we left. We prayed silently and hoped someone would open the gate and help us.

As we sat in prayer we could hear the commotion all around us. People screaming and crying, hurrying in every direction. Just then we heard a voice from below.

"YOU THERE! On deck NOW!"

I turned and looked down only to see George's bright blue eyes looking back at me.

"Bridget!"

"George!" I exclaimed.

"We're lost and the gates are locked. Please help us."

He motioned for us to follow him and we did. He directed us to another stairwell on the opposite end of the Second Class Library and up we went.

We continued to follow him up to the Bridge Deck and then the Promenade Deck. As we finally reached the Boat Deck we noticed the boats being lowered. Number 15 had just gone over the side by the time we arrived.

"Come!" yelled George.

"We can still make 15 from the A-Deck!"

We followed him back down the stairwell to the Promenade Deck as the boat continued to be lowered. It had already passed us by, but George urged us to jump. James knew he wouldn't be able to join us as the order was for women and children only.

"Don't worry about me," he said. "I'll find you. I promise."

The distance between the deck and the lifeboat seemed overwhelming. I didn't feel we could make it. Just then George jumped in the boat.

Coming to his feet he raised his arms and yelled, "JUMP!"

CHAPTER 8

RMS *Titanic*
April 15, 1912

Staring down at the boat below and then over to Helen, I motioned for her to jump. I followed after she jumped and landed between the seats of an already crowded lifeboat. I felt a sharp pain rise from my legs through my low back and winced in agony. As the boat was lowered I heard the sailors shout,

"Lower aft! Lower stern! Lower together!"

Slowly the boat which was filled to capacity with terrified passengers glided down the side of the ship. Helen and I stood together as George and the other crewman onboard tried to keep everyone calm.

Below us was Lifeboat 13 which had been lowered just moments before ours. When it reached the sea it was drawn back towards the hull by water flowing from the condenser. We seemed to be approaching the water rather quickly. Down, down we went until we heard screams from below.

"STOP!" yelled the voices of those aboard.

Realizing we were approaching too rapidly, George and the others aboard our boat yelled back to the Bridge Deck for our boat to stop, but apparently their pleas went unnoticed and we continued down. Finally we were nearly on top of them when one of the sailors aboard Lifeboat 13 pulled out his knife and released the boat which flung out of the way allowing our boat to land in its place.

"Wow, close call," mumbled George.

There were a number of crew aboard our boat and they took charge to level the boat and then row away from the *Titanic*. Some of the sailors had mentioned the possible threat of a large wave emerging should the mighty ship sink, so they tried to row as fast as they could away from the ship. Nearly an hour had passed when the lights from the *Titanic* began to flicker and then finally went out. It was a somber moment for all of us. As we stood there trying to comprehend what was happening, I spotted young Charlie in his mother's arms as the other boys clung to her dress. My heart broke fearing they would not survive should *Titanic* sink, and I felt so helpless in that moment.

All of the sudden we heard two explosions and then a collective sigh as the mighty ship seemed to break in two. George explained how the stern end of the ship contained all of the engines and turbine, and how the weight of it was so great the hull could not support it. The bow section of the ship, which was full of water, was pulled towards the seabed due to gravity. Just then the entire ship slowly began to sink to its murky grave at the bottom of the sea. At that moment I swore I heard the band playing, and thought of what I had left behind in my cabin, a beautiful painting and my book. They were now lost forever, yet that did not matter much.

The moments that followed were nearly unbearable. Those who weren't able to make the lifeboats had now plunged into the sea and were fighting for their lives. What started out as screams for help soon became moans and gasps of air as hypothermia began to set in. I wanted so much to help but our boat was already full and we simply couldn't go back to rescue anyone. Some of the women on our boat became hysterical and pleaded with the sailors to return to take on more passengers.

As we stood in the lifeboat, gathered together like a bunch of sardines, I began to feel faint. The pain in my back had increased and I needed to sit down. I began to lean back and felt a pair of arms grab me. It was Helen.

"Are you okay?" she asked.

"I need to sit," I replied.

I thought I would become sick to my stomach and

reached for the edge of the boat, my hair dangling in the sea. Suddenly my eyes became fixed on a set of portholes and I watched until they disappeared below the surface. It was an agonizing feeling; so helpless and yet relief that I was in a lifeboat and not on the ship.

The time on the lifeboat seemed surreal and I had to imagine myself someplace else just to cope. I knew how lucky I was to be alive, yet I wondered if we'd be rescued in time. The bitter cold was something fierce and most of us were not equipped with enough clothing to keep us warm. Although I was able to put on my coat, my fingers were becoming numb and the only thing that kept me in a state of reality were the warm sting of tears that glided slowly down my cheeks from time to time.

George and the other sailors kept yelling directions to keep our boat level. Some of the other passengers helped row as well. I sat there watching George at work, somehow remaining calm throughout the chaos. As he was guiding us through the ship he was very stern in his approach, instructing us to follow or die. I was frightened yet confident that he would help us reach the boats in time. Once the *Titanic* sunk we were left with very little light except for the stars that lit up the sky. There appeared to be thousands, and I couldn't help but keep my gaze upon them. We wondered if any rescue ships would spot us. Some of the sailors lit small green flares to make themselves known in the vast sea.

Once the *Titanic* had sunk the sea was filled with debris along with bodies. Furnishings and pieces of clothing were spotted around where the mighty ship once lay. I looked down to see suitcases and pieces of splintered wood, some with strands of jewelry that managed to attach themselves, floating in the water. Yet I was too cold to move. I wondered who the pieces of jewelry belonged to and had they survived? I thought of the blue heart and how happy the woman wearing it had appeared. Did she manage to survive, and what had become of her fiancé? Time seemed to stand still and I would get lost in my mind trying to imagine different surroundings. Every once and a while I would be shaken back to reality by a gasp or shriek from a fellow passenger.

On occasion we would see another lifeboat close in to our location and the sailors would yell back and forth status reports. I was feeling a bit better sitting down, although I wasn't really sure if it meant my injuries weren't serious, or if it was just the cold having numbed my limbs. I couldn't really feel my legs anymore and tried not to make any sudden moves. I put my hand to my chest and thought of the cross necklace secured around my neck. I prayed we would remain safe and be rescued in time. I thought of Robert and our life that awaited us in New York. We were just beginning our lives and it couldn't possibly end like this.

The time in the lifeboat seemed as though it would go on forever. The cries we heard after the great ship sank lasted about twenty minutes yet lingered in my ears. George would glance over occasionally and our eyes would meet with a look of both concern and relief. It was a horrific circumstance, yet we were alive and that was where our focus needed to remain. Our hopes would be lifted momentarily as we spotted lights in the distance, only to be dashed when informed it was just another lifeboat. The sailors continued to set off flares and provide some type of light in hopes we would be spotted.

Finally around 3:30 am we spotted what appeared to be a bright light in the distance. I asked George if it was a vessel coming to our rescue and he replied that it must be a ship's light. Suddenly two bright green lights broke through the mist and one of the sailors yelled, "It's a ship!" I put my hand to my heart again, feeling for my cross and thanking God for looking after us. Many of those from our boat began yelling,

"WE ARE SAVED!"

CHAPTER 9

Lily

Coronado, California
April, 2012

The visit to the *Titanic* exhibit must have triggered something in my subconscious mind as the dream had returned last night. I was jolted awake with a sense of both terror and relief that it had returned. In some way it had become such a staple of my existence that when it left me, I felt lost. I was curious once again as to discover its meaning, and find a way to move forward. I also thought about the woman I had met yesterday from the exhibit. She had played the role of a *Titanic* passenger so well, that speaking with her made me feel as though we had been transported back to 1912. She spoke with such passion about the great ship and her dream of coming to America from Ireland. In a way I felt as though I was part of her journey.

While I was at the newspaper office yesterday TJ had given me a few back issues of the *Gazette* to look over. He felt it would provide me with a better sense of the community and serve as a good way to learn more about Coronado and what took place here on the island. While reading one of the issues I came across the story of a local man, Brian Jackson, who had recovered the silver coins from the gambling ship, *S.S. Monte Carlo* that had beached itself on our shores. Apparently he found $410,000 worth of silver coins and had been planning the recovery for some time.

The winter storms that hit the area proved useful to the local who apparently had been planning the recovery mission since he was a boy. The *S.S. Monte Carlo* was originally an oil tanker launched in 1921, which then became a gambling ship anchored three miles off the coast of Coronado in 1936. It had sailed down from Long Beach where it shared international waters with other gambling ships. On New Year's Eve in 1936, it broke free from its anchor lines due to a fierce storm and ran aground just south of the famed Hotel del Coronado. Today, the remnants of the ship remain visible during negative low tides.

It was truly a fascinating read and I was anxious to explore the area to see if I could spot the ship. Who knows? Perhaps I could possibly find a treasure of my own. I decided to check online to view the tide calendar to see when the next negative low tide would occur. As luck would have it, it was this week, and tomorrow morning appeared to be the perfect time to go beachcombing. I spent the rest of the day surfing the net to learn as much as I could about the gambling ship.

What I found in my research was quite fascinating. Apparently "sin ships" as they were known back then, were quite the rave in the 1930s. Although gambling was illegal in California, the state's jurisdiction only reached three miles off the coast which then was considered international waters. There was no federal law prohibiting gambling, so all floating gambling casinos had to do was anchor just outside the three mile limit. Gambling quickly became quite profitable, and by 1930 there was a small fleet of these ships off the coast of California between Santa Monica and Long Beach.

One of the most famous of these sin ships was the *S.S. Rex* which was launched in 1938 by Tony Cornero. Its popularity came about due to the fact it catered to middle class clientele rather than the high rollers. It operated twenty-four hours a day and welcomed between 1,000 to 3,000 gamblers at any given time. There were numerous attempts by local law enforcement to shut down the ships, but their hands were always tied due to jurisdiction issues. The *S.S. Rex* would continue to operate until it was finally sent off to serve in war efforts during World War II.

After reading up about these vessels online, I decided to head out for a walk. I strolled up Orange Avenue towards the ocean. I walked passed the Hotel del Coronado and south down the beach path. As I approached the area that was flagged off to warn about the ship, I noticed the signs but didn't see any remnants of the boat. I hoped to have better luck tomorrow morning. I knew I would need to wake early, but I was excited to see if I could spot her. I have always been fascinated by history, and my love/hate relationship with the ocean would once again be tested.

The following morning I woke around 4:00 am. I couldn't sleep due to a combination of thinking about the *S.S. Monte Carlo*, and my dream that decided two days in a row it was necessary to reappear in my subconscious mind. It made me think perhaps the two were connected somehow. I lay in bed contemplating the possibility. It was still dark when I left the house at 5:15 am. It took me about a half hour to walk to the shipwreck. There was some lighting from the Shores condominium complex casting a low glow on the beach, but it wasn't bright enough to illuminate anything in great detail. I thought I spotted some remnants of the ship and headed down to the sand for a closer look.

The beach was empty as I made my way down to the shoreline. I wore my rubber soled beach shoes to protect my feet from any sharp edges I might encounter, and had brought my camera in hopes of capturing some images of the vessel. As I walked closer I began to notice some different shaped mounds of material covered in algae and seaweed. I captured a few images and then was startled momentary by a voice.

"Hey there! Be careful!"

I looked over to see a young man approaching from the south. As he grew closer I noticed he was quite handsome with dark hair and piercing blue eyes. He wore a black sweat suit, running shoes and a baseball cap.

As I moved back from the wreckage he approached me. It was about 6:15 am at this point and the sky had cleared to display specks of pink hue on the horizon to welcome the sunrise. It also provided a better view of the stranger.

"Oh, I'm sorry," I said as I continued to back away.

Just then I noticed the tide begin to change and the waves moved over the wreckage with a stronger intensity. Before long it was no longer visible.

"Sorry, didn't mean to startle you. The waves shift rather quickly and you have to be careful. I'm David. I run this beach every morning so I've seen how quickly it can change."

I smiled and thanked him for his concern.

"I'm Lily. I'm new in town and had heard about the wreckage. I was just hoping to check it out."

He motioned for me to follow him back to the walking path where we sat on one of the benches.

He extended his hand, shook mine, and smiled.

"Nice to meet you, Lily. I'm one of the local guards and we're always warning the public to be cautious around the vessel. It can be dangerous if you're not familiar with the tides."

I shook my head in agreement and thanked him again. As I removed my shoes and dried off my feet with my towel, we continued to chat. He shared more about himself and a bit about Coronado that he thought I might enjoy. He was twenty-three years old and in his first full year as an ocean lifeguard. He was from Los Angeles and had a business degree from a small private university, yet he loved the sea. After completing the training to be a lifeguard in Los Angeles he decided he much rather prefer the low key lifestyle that the island could provide. His family had moved to San Diego and he preferred being closer to them as they were a very tight knit family.

He shared how Coronado was a great community and how I would love living here. I expressed how I, too, was from LA, and had come down here on several occasions over the years to get away from the hustle and bustle of the big city. I shared with him my passion for writing and photography, and he told me that he also enjoyed both, especially photography. For some reason I felt so comfortable talking with him that I decided to tell him what was going on with my dream, and how it was that which led me to make the move here to Coronado. He smiled and shared he had a similar dream a few years back when he was at university, and perhaps that was one of the reasons he chose to become a lifeguard instead of pursuing a career in business. He said that in the dream he saw people struggling in the sea and felt so helpless, not being able to help. Now he could.

I also expressed how much I loved the sea and yet had what I considered a love/hate relationship with it. I loved to swim, but would only do so in pools. And although I loved being near the sea and would go near it, I wouldn't swim in the ocean. I expressed how this fear had paralyzed me for so long and now I felt I needed to somehow find a way to overcome it. He was very sweet and said that sometimes we have to take leaps of faith in life to reach our full potential, and that my fear of the sea may not be as strong as I was making it out to be. He also assured me that if I ever did decide to go into the ocean that he would be there to support me.

I told him about the *Titanic* exhibit and how I was able to help out the *Gazette* the other day with covering the Centennial celebrations. He asked how I enjoyed the exhibit and I told him I had loved it. Actually very much so, and that I had even gone back yesterday for another viewing. He laughed and said that was great. He then mentioned that he was reluctantly going to the Centennial Dinner on Saturday with his parents, and that he didn't really want to go.

"Really?" I asked.

"I would love to go."

He smiled as his eyes grew wide.

"Do you want to come along? My Dad was given tickets through work. We have four tickets, but only can use three. I'm sure my folks wouldn't mind, and you'd be saving me the agony of having to sit there alone in my own misery."

I returned his wide-eyed glance and shook my head in agreement.

"Are you sure though? I mean, we just met and all and don't you have a girlfriend or someone else you'd rather take?"

He smiled and assured me it would be fine, then stood and extended his hand again.

"Well, it was great meeting you, Lily. I have to wrap up my work-out before my shift begins. I'll text you my contact information and details on the dinner."

"Okay, thanks. Here is my business card with my info," I replied.

I was thrilled and excited. I normally didn't accept invitations from strangers I just met, but there was something different about him. I felt very comfortable around him, as if I knew him somehow. I wrapped my wet shoes in my towel, threw on my flip flops and walked home.

Once there I began to think about the Centennial dinner and what I could possibly wear. With a ticket price of $212.00, I was sure jeans and a t-shirt just wouldn't cut it. I opened my closet and started searching the back corner where I kept a few cocktail dresses. I found a simple black dress that I felt would be suitable. If only I could wear my everyday sandals. I really didn't mind dressing up, and it was fun every now and then, yet I was much more comfortable in loose clothing and bare feet. I also needed to figure out what to do with my hair, as tying it up in the simple pony tail wouldn't do. I had two days to work with so I decided to call Kate. She was always attending parties and events in LA and would know what to do.

About an hour later, the phone rang. It was Kate returning my call.

"You've met someone and you're going where? What's going on girl?" she practically yelled into the phone.

I laughed and shared my adventures of the last few days and how I was so excited to go to this dinner, yet didn't really know how to dress. She assured me she'd help me put together the perfect look. She agreed the black dress was a great choice and I would need to wear clear stockings and my black heels. I could compliment the dress with my pearl earrings and necklace. That would make it look classy and presentable. With only two days to prepare, I really didn't have time to accommodate the 1912 fashion style, but I would make do with what I had.

The following day I decided to visit the library which was a short walk from my home. As I entered the building I was pleasantly surprised by its beauty and vast space. I checked in at the reception desk and mentioned I was just visiting. The woman who greeted me welcomed me and gave me a brief background of the space. The library was housed in a 40,000 square foot building that had a little bit of everything for everyone. There were study areas that comprised of tables and chairs as well as lounge seating. Meeting rooms, both large and small, were scattered about as well as a special area for children and also one for teens. A beautiful exhibit gallery, a public-access computer room, and even a used book store completed the space. I had never experienced a library like this one and immediately fell in love with it. As I walked around taking in each area I also noticed that one of the study areas that housed tables and chairs looked out over a bowling green. WOW! I was impressed.

After my self-guided tour I inquired about books on Coronado's history, especially those that had information on the Monte Carlo shipwreck. I was given a couple books about Coronado and found a table in the front lounge area to sit and spread out the material.

There wasn't much information on the shipwreck, but what I found was pretty fascinating and my excitement and curiosity continued to grow. I wondered what secrets this shipwreck held, and what adventures lie ahead with my new friend David.

CHAPTER 10

Coronado, California
April 14, 2012

Today was the big day - the day of the Centennial dinner at Prado restaurant in Balboa Park. I was so excited and hardly slept last night in anticipation of the evening ahead. I was also a little nervous to see David again and meet his parents. I was curious to see their reaction to David inviting someone he had just met to this fancy dinner. I decided to just play it cool and figured everything would be fine. Dinner was slated to begin at 6:00 pm and David said he would pick me up at 5:30 pm. I hung up my dress and placed the other items out for easy access for when it was time to get ready.

Most of the day was spent looking over the material I had picked up from the library and once again checking the tide calendar online to see when would be a good time to view the *Monte Carlo*. It appeared tomorrow would be ideal, but again early in the morning. I figured this time I would go a bit earlier and take a small flashlight to help me spot the vessel. I really wanted to capture some good photos and I had learned how quickly the tides could change when I was there the other day. I figured I wouldn't have much time so I needed to make the most of it.

I also knew I probably wouldn't get much sleep tonight depending on what time the dinner finished and what time I would actually get home. Plus I was sure that I'd be too excited to sleep. Oh well. I was determined to see the shipwreck and it wasn't as if it was a daily occurrence. I did manage to get through last night without the dream popping up in my head so I was happy about that. I was also determined to get to the bottom of whatever the dream was trying to tell me, although now I was quite curious to learn more about David's dream that he mentioned having a few years back. He had said it was similar to mine yet didn't go into great detail.

At 5:00 pm I finished applying my makeup and slipped into the black cocktail dress I had left hanging on my closet door. I put on my pearl earrings and placed the pearl necklace around my neck. I put a few things into a small black purse and grabbed my gray jacket from the closet. I was ready and excited for David to arrive. At 5:30 pm sharp I received a text message that he had arrived. I opened the door to find him walking up the pathway to my apartment. He looked so different dressed in a dark suit, navy blue shirt, and a dark tie.

"WOW! You look amazing," he said as he approached the door.

"Thank you. You look pretty great yourself," I replied.

"Ha! Thanks. I feel as though I'm wearing a strait jacket."

We both laughed.

He took my hand and led me to his car, a black Ford SUV. He opened the passenger door and closed it behind me after I entered. He then went around to the driver's side and entered the vehicle.

"Ready for this circus act?" he asked with a wink of his eye.

"Ha! I'm sure it won't be all that terrible," I replied.

The drive across the bridge took no time and we arrived at Prado restaurant shortly before 6:00 pm. As we entered the Grand Ballroom we were greeted by a wait staff wearing white period tuxedo jackets. We were then seated at a table where David's parents, Marjorie and John greeted us.

"It's a pleasure to meet you, dear," offered Marjorie with her hand extended.

"Thank you both for having me," I replied, and shook her hand. "It was very nice of David to invite me, seeing that we had just met."

"Well, our son has a way with the ladies," echoed John with a smile on his face.

"Dad, please. You don't want to scare her away before we've even sat down."

"Sorry son."

David pulled out the chair in front of me and offered me the seat.

"Why thank you, kind sir," I said as I sat down.

Once we were all seated we were greeted again by the wait staff who welcomed us to the event. On each place setting lay a menu of the ten-course dinner that awaited us, the same that was served to the First Class passengers aboard the *Titanic* on their final night before she struck the iceberg. We were then served the first wine pairing of the evening; a Chablis which we were told came from the Burgundy region of France and was made from one hundred percent of Chardonnay grapes. I'm not a big wine drinker, so passed on being offered a glass as did David, so we just learned of each pairing through our server as well as his parents who enjoyed different variations. They had taken a taxi to the affair so neither of them had to drive home after the event.

The first course consisted of raw oysters and although I wasn't a big fan of shelled fish, I did try a couple. David was happy to finish his entire portion.

"Yummy! What's next?" he said with a big smile on his face.

We both laughed.

"So Lily," Marjorie interrupted. "David says you are new to San Diego?"

"Yes. I recently moved down from LA. I graduated from USC a few years ago and was working for a local paper in Santa Monica, but felt it was time for a fresh start. I'm a photographer, but I'd love to write for a newspaper down here. I have a friend who works for the *Gazette* and he invited me here to shoot the opening of Centennial Week. That is how I learned of the exhibit and all that was planned for the week."

"Fantastic!" she replied.

"And as luck would have it, you bumped into

David on the beach?" added John.

David looked over and winked as I returned a smile.

"Lucky me!" I replied.

It was then time for the second course to arrive. We were served Consommé Olga, a clear soup made by adding a mixture of ground meats together with a combination of carrots, celery, and onion, parsley, tomatoes, and egg whites into beef stock, then strained. It was quite tasty and I enjoyed it thoroughly. David seemed to as well as he appeared to inhale the contents of the bowl in front of him.

I tried not to laugh as I looked over to his expression of complete satisfaction as he spooned the last of it.

"Did you enjoy that? I asked.

"OH YES! Next!" he replied with a big grin on his face.

We both chuckled quietly and then straightened our expressions as we caught the suspicious look from David's father whose eyes had narrowed as he gave him a stern look. The wait staff then approached with the second wine pairing for the evening, a dry Riesling from the Rhine region of Germany.

"Remember John, this is what was served on the river cruise we took last summer when we visited Europe?" said Marjorie as she took a sip from her glass.

"Oh yes," replied John. "It's a bit too sweet for my liking."

David nodded his head in agreement and then his eyes grew wide as the wait staff approached with the third course.

"Poached salmon with mousseline sauce. Enjoy."

"Oh, my favorite!" replied David as he held up his knife and fork in either hand, ready to dig in.

I, on the other hand wasn't as thrilled. I'd never been a big fan of salmon and remembered the first and only time I had experienced the dish. I was on holiday in the Burgundy region of France and staying at a beautiful chateau. After one bite I remember thinking, "Where's dessert?" I had stared down at the plate with the salmon placed in the center with a yellow crème sauce on top and some cucumber on the side. I love cucumber so I dipped them in the sauce and pretended to enjoy the side dish.

Instead of inhaling the dish as he had with the soup, David took small bites as if to savor every one.

"Aren't you glad we came Lily? I'm really enjoying this feast much more than I thought I would," asked David.

"Ha! Yes. I think I'm enjoying watching your reaction to the food rather than the meal itself, but I'm enjoying it for sure. Thanks again for inviting me."

David smiled and continued to finish off the plate of salmon.

"So what are your plans now that you've found a place to live here, Lily?" asked John.

"Well, the *Gazette* offered me some freelance work as a photographer until I can find something more permanent. I'm also quite fascinated with the S.S. *Monte Carlo* and the story that surrounds the shipwreck.

"Oh yes! Did you hear the news about the BIG find, the recovery of the silver coins?"

"Yes, I was reading the back issues of the *Gazette*. Quite a story. Apparently Mr. Jackson had been planning the recovery since he was a boy."

"Yep, he's quite the character, that Brian," added David.

When it was time for the fourth course, David rubbed his stomach and smiled.

"Wow! I haven't eaten this well, in... well forever."

The wait staff approached the table with the next course and I smiled this time relieved it wasn't another seafood platter. Instead, we were served Filet Mignon Lili and a sauté of Chicken Lyonnaise with a vegetable marrow farcie. It looked and smelled divine. I was also really hungry by this point after sampling bits of the last three courses. This time it was I who took my time with each piece I placed in my mouth to savor the amazing flavor of the dish. When the wait staff came to collect our plates, the young man looked at me and smiled, obviously happy to see I enjoyed at least one of the courses. I certainly didn't want it to get back to the Executive Chef that his dishes were a bust. God forbid!

As I sat reflecting on the delicious meal, I realized I was feeling quite full. I became a bit nervous that we were only halfway through the banquet and that I wouldn't be able to finish all the dishes. I looked over at David who appeared quite content to eat all night long. I did wonder where he put it all as his thin frame looked quite dashing in his suit.

"Good thing I'm not scheduled to work tomorrow," he said as he rubbed his stomach again. "They might have to roll me out of here."

I laughed at the image I envisioned in my head. "Ha! You and me both," I replied.

The wait staff returned, this time with the third wine pairing, a light Beaujolais which was the first of the red wines served so far.

"It's a French wine, again from the Burgundy region that comes from the Gamay grape, or purple grape. They are usually used to make red wines," added John as he took a sip from his glass.

The wait staff then returned with the fifth course, lamb with mint sauce accompanied by a green pea puree, and Parmentier potatoes.

"Wow! That looks divine as well, although I'm not sure how much more my stomach can handle. This is indeed a feast."

David simply smiled and grabbed his utensils in either hand as if he was in the running for some sort of state fair all-you-can-eat contest. I couldn't help but giggle at his sheer delight with every dish that was presented before him.

The lamb was delicious but now I was completely full. There was no way I was going to be able to eat anymore, although the sixth course looked interesting – Punch Romaine Cocktail. I stared at the menu card for a moment trying to think of what it could possibly be. At least it wasn't food.

"Ah yes, time for the cleanser," said John with a smile on his face.

"Cleanser?" I asked.

"Oh yes, the Punch Cocktail. It's a lovely treat of crushed ice with just a touch of rum. Delicious! It was made famous by French chef Georges Escoffier in the early twentieth century."

Just as John was describing the drink, the wait staff arrived with one for each of us. It was a nice looking cocktail, orange and white in color with an orange peel serving as a garnish.

"Oh! This looks nice. What else is in it?" I asked.

The wait staff decided to answer. "Along with crushed ice, we create a simple syrup along with champagne, white wine, orange juice and lemon juice, as well as a little bit of rum."

"Sounds yummy," I added. "I think I will try some.

"I'll pass," David replied. "After all, I'm driving us home."

I drank about half of it and it was yummy, but I didn't want to overload my system with alcohol since I didn't drink much at all. David and I had been drinking water all evening and that seemed fine with him as well.

The wait staff then returned with the seventh course of the evening, roast squab on watercress. It was served with the fourth wine pairing, a red burgundy.

"What is squab?" I asked

"Um, chicken?" David replied with a sly grin on his face.

I looked at him as my eyes narrowed. "Somehow I think you're pulling my leg," I responded. "Although it doesn't really matter. I can't eat another bite."

"Well then, it's actually a young pigeon. You know, those flying rats you see at the beach all the time?"

"Awwww, that's cruel." I replied as I envisioned

being surrounded by pigeons on the beach. I could never bring myself to look at one again if I ate one.

"That's okay, I'll pass," I said pushing the plate away.

David continued eating as if he didn't have a care in the world. Once again I was amazed at all he had eaten and we weren't even done yet. By the time the eighth course came I was actually feeling better. Apparently the punch cleanse really worked. I didn't feel as full as I had after finishing the Filet Mignon. The wait staff approached and served us cold asparagus with a champagne-saffron vinaigrette. I actually decided to take a bite and it was pretty good.

When the wait staff returned with the ninth course I was thinking we should be close to dessert, but that wasn't the case. Instead we were served pâté de foie gras which was fat goose liver.

"I think I'll pass," I said looking down at the plate. "I keep envisioning all those poor birds."

David simply smiled and carved out a piece with his knife. "Don't mind if I do, thank you," he replied.

I gave him a slight smile and took another drink of water. The wine selection that accompanied the course was a Sauternes, a French sweet wine from the region of Bordeaux. David's parents seemed to enjoy the different variations and reminisced on their travels abroad throughout the evening.

"We're almost to the finish line," said David with a big smile on his face.

"I simply don't know where you put it all," I replied.

Rubbing his stomach with both hands, he exclaimed, "Who's ready for dessert?"

Just as he finished the sentence the wait staff approached with a tray of the most scrumptious desserts I had seen. Waldorf pudding, chocolate eclairs, and peaches in chartreuse jelly.

"Oh wow!" I added.

We each decided to take our time with dessert, placing each bite slowly in our mouths and savoring the delicious flavor. There was very little said as we ate. Then when we were all finished we simply sunk down a bit in our chairs and admired the feast we had just experienced.

"Well, I think we should do this at least once a month, eh Dad?" suggested David.

"Ha! You would!" replied John with a hearty laugh.

At the conclusion of dinner we took a moment to enjoy the piano quintet that had been playing era-specific melodies from 1912 throughout the evening. They were quite good and certain pieces felt as though they were transporting us back in time.

"Well, your mother and I are off David," said John as he rose from the table and took hold of Marjorie's chair.

"Oh, you're not staying to view the exhibit?" replied David.

"No, we'll pass. It's here for a while so I'm sure we'll see it at some point. It's been a long day and we're both tired." Marjorie nodded her head in agreement.

"It was a pleasure to meet you, Lily," said Marjorie, as she extended her hand.

"Yes, you both as well, and thank you again so much for including me this evening. I really enjoyed myself."

After giving David a hug and pat on the shoulder by his father, they both headed out of the ballroom.

"Would you like to stay and view the exhibit again, Lily? I know you've already seen it, but I thought it might be fun to see it together," asked David.

"Absolutely! I'd love to."

I collected my coat and we were directed by the staff out of the ballroom and restaurant to the walkway which led to the Natural History Museum. It was a short walk and a beautiful starlit night. We arrived at the museum and showed our dinner passes which included a visit to view the exhibit. The museum had extended its hours tonight specifically for dinner guests until 3:00 am. This way guests could view the exhibit at the exact hour in which the *Titanic* sank one hundred years ago.

As we walked through the exhibit, there were moments when I would glance over at David and catch him with an expression on his face as if he were deep in thought. I didn't want to break his concentration, but wondered what he must have been feeling. I know the impact the exhibit had on me the first time I saw it as well as the second time. The flashes from my reoccurring dream that had returned when visiting certain areas made me question if there was indeed a connection between the two.

I also thought about what David had said about his own dream and was curious to learn more. As we approached the Third Class accommodations and I saw the bunk beds again, a familiar feeling filled my being once again.

"Hmmm, I wonder," I quietly whispered.

"Wonder what?" asked David.

"Oh, the bunk beds. I've seen this room now three times and it always brings about a feeling of familiarity."

"Hmmm, I know what you mean. I was just thinking the same thing, but I chalked it up to the memory of all my international travels when I stayed in hostels," replied David.

"Oh yes, I've done that as well, but I don't know. This somehow feels different."

David shrugged his shoulders and replied, "I guess."

"Hey. Speaking of which, David, you mentioned you had a similar dream a few years back. What was that all about if you don't mind me asking?"

"Well, I don't really remember much about it, only

that I was on the water in a boat of some sort. I just remember the sounds more than anything."

"What kind of sounds?" I asked.

"Well, not sure really. Moans, screams, calls for help. I just felt so helpless. I wanted to help yet for some reason I wasn't able to. I just can't figure out why and what it meant."

"Wow! That sounds a lot like the dream I've been having of late."

"Really?" replied David.

"Yeah. It started a couple months ago I guess, but of late it just seemed so vivid as if I were there. Freaked me out. I've had it a couple times since arriving here in San Diego, but I just don't understand what it means."

"I suppose we both have a mystery on our hands," added David.

"Yes, I suppose so."

We continued touring the exhibit and an announcement was made by one of the staff that we were approaching the hour of *Titanic's* sinking, and would we please all gather in an area where a band was playing *"Nearer My God to Thee."* David took my hand and we followed the others into the rotunda. There was a small group playing violins and the women sang the tune as everyone gathered together. Halfway through the song I felt a chill go up my spine and I looked at David.

"I think we've had enough," he said as he reached for my hand.

"I agree," I replied.

We turned around and headed for the exit. As the cool air hit our faces once we stepped outside, I looked at David.

"You felt it too, didn't you?" I asked.

"Yes, chills. I just knew we had to get out of there. I can't really explain why though."

I didn't understand why either. We headed to the car and he opened the passenger door to let me in. I sat in silence thinking of what we had just experienced. David entered the car and fastened his seatbelt. The drive back to Coronado was quiet. Neither of us knew what to say. It was close to 3:00 am when we arrived at my apartment. David exited the car and opened my door for me to get out.

"Thank you, and thanks again for a lovely

evening. Um, I didn't really know what to say."

Placing his right index finger on my lips, he smiled. "Neither do I, and it's okay. Thank you for joining me tonight."

I smiled as he walked me to my door.

"Good night."

"Good night, David, and thanks again."

After undressing and putting my black sweat pants and a T-shirt on, I sat down on my bed and grabbed my journal from the night stand. I opened it up and wrote down the date – *APRIL 14, 2012. Oh what a day!*

After writing down all I had experienced from preparing for the event, meeting David's parents, the incredible feast, and the uncomfortable feeling we both felt at the exhibit when the band had played that song, I sat for a moment in silence.

"What if there is some kind of connection?" I said softly to myself as I read over my words. "What if our dreams are not simply dreams, but memories?"

CHAPTER 11
Bridget

RMS *Titanic*
April 15, 1912

Several moments passed as we watched in anticipation as the great ship grew closer. Some of the passengers burned newspapers, personal letters, and handkerchiefs to signal the ship to our location. The sailors also continued to shoot off what remaining green flares they had available. Shortly after 4:00 am the ship had reached the first lifeboat. We were still quite a distance from the ship and the sailors worked hard to row us in. As dawn approached we noticed we were floating in an iceberg field. There was a very large iceberg that separated us from the rescue ship and we had to row around it which took time.

The hours passed as we continued to row towards the rescue ship. Our lifeboat was nearly filled to capacity and took somewhat more effort on the part of the sailors to maneuver through the sea and iceberg field. We were amazed at the sight of so much ice and the vast size of some of the bergs we passed. It certainly explained the bitter cold air throughout the night. Strands of my hair that had fallen in the sea before we became level were now frozen from the cold. The numbness throughout my lower body was such that I knew I wouldn't be able to stand on my own.

As we grew closer to the rescue ship one of the sailors shouted out,

"It's the *Carpathia*!"

There was a cheer that went up between us, grateful for our rescuer. We noticed passengers from the ship looking down on us as we approached. Once our lifeboat reached the ship around 7:30 am, the *Carpathia's* crew went straight to work. They had positioned ladders over the side of the ship and ropes were also lowered down to the water. Chair slings were also provided to support the children and the injured as they were lifted up to the deck. One by one the passengers from our boat were taken aboard the *Carpathia*. George came over and picked me up in his arms as another sailor secured a rope around my body which then hoisted me to the deck. I couldn't feel my legs but there was very little pain. It was more like a numbness had settled in my limbs.

Once on board the *Carpathia* we were taken to one of the dining saloons that had been turned into a makeshift hospital. There we were provided with blankets and doctors looked after us. A young woman approached and handed me a hot drink. The liquid felt so good as it made its way through my body, and before long the sensations returned in my fingers as I held on to the cup. I lay down on my back on a stretcher and a doctor looked me over, explaining how lucky I was. He stated I didn't have any broken bones but there was inflammation in the area of my sacrum which would subside with rest. This would explain for the loss of feeling in my legs and hopefully I would be okay by the time we reached New York.

Before long I looked up to see Helen approaching.

"Helen!" I exclaimed.

"Bridget! I'm so glad you are okay. Look who I found!"

I looked over her shoulder to see James coming up behind her, a blanket across his shoulders, his face pale.

"Oh James! You're okay. Thank God!"

We all joined hands and breathed a sigh of relief.

The *Carpathia* was a huge ship similar to *Titanic* and could hold more than two thousand passengers.

Yet there were only about eight hundred on board we were told when they rescued us. The empty berths were used to house the majority of the First and Second class passengers. Those of us from steerage were taken to areas of the promenade where makeshift beds were made to accommodate us. Other areas such as the smoking rooms, library and some of the officer's cabins were also used to accommodate our passengers.

Prior to retreating to the promenade we were provided with bowls of soup and more hot drinks to help our bodies recover. I was so impressed by the stewards and crew that went out of their way to make sure we had everything we needed. Some of *Carpathia's* passengers were even so kind as to craft makeshift clothing out of burlap sacks which they provided to some passengers who desperately needed a change of clothing.

"Have you seen George?" I asked Helen.

"No, but I'm sure he's just attending to other passengers. I'm almost certain he's fine and you'll see him before long."

I wanted to thank him again, as if it weren't for him, we might have never reached the lifeboats in time.

By 9:00 am the last of the passengers from the lifeboats had been rescued and *Carpathia* began its journey back to New York. We had learned she left New York on Thursday and was heading to Fiume, Austria-Hungary with a ship filled with mostly tourists. We were so grateful to the passengers who offered help and thanked them for being so gracious in their understanding considering the way their holidays were interrupted. Everyone was so nice and it was comforting.

Most of the morning was spent watching the crew help those who were injured, and also assisting families in searching for loved ones. It was agonizing watching some of the women and children when told their husbands and fathers had not survived. Some women broke down near the rails of the ship as they wailed in sorrow for their loved ones. The stewards did all they could to comfort them, yet the look of distraught wore like a veil upon their faces.

There were quite a few of the crew from the Engine Room on our lifeboat and many lost friends who remained with the *Titanic*, trying to keep her afloat. George had mentioned that he was just about to begin his shift when he was instructed to support the stewards in guiding those of us from the bottom of the ship to the Boat Deck. I'm not sure what we would have done had he not appeared just when we needed him. The chaos that had surrounded us lay cemented in my memory. The cries from the sea I desperately hoped to release from my mind but to no avail. Although we were now safely on board another ship, I could not rest without worry. I would not feel safe again until we reached land.

The afternoon arrived as most of us were now housed on deck and could easily tell what time of day it was. Blankets wrapped our bodies and stewards approached with trays of food for us. We hadn't had a full meal since supper the day before and the food was certainly welcomed. I knew I needed to regain my energy if I were to make a full recovery from my injuries. I was lucky that it wasn't worse. I was sure I had broken a bone when I made the jump into the lifeboat, but I did not. Just the strain on my back lingered which I knew would heal in time. I needed to make sure I didn't overexert myself. We were told it would take three days to reach New York and I decided I would rest as much I could in that time.

Helen and James joined me as we ate bread and cups of soup. James shared how he managed to make it to one of the collapsible lifeboats after jumping into the water from *Titanic's* deck.

"It was nearly 2:30 am and all of the boats had been launched. The *Titanic* began to sink. I had just hit the water and my body had not reacted well to the bitter temperatures. I knew I needed to get out of the water or I would certainly die."

We were all so relieved and gathered hands in a prayer of gratitude.

As we were finishing our meal I spotted George and called for him. He came over immediately and asked us all if we needed anything. We assured him we were okay and he then excused himself saying he needed to attend to the others. He was certainly a hero to me and to so many others I was sure. Although I learned he was a couple years younger than me, he acted very mature. He was direct in his actions and instructions, yet had a calm presence about him that made me feel safe. There was never a sense of panic with George. He knew what needed to be done and went about doing his job the best he could, considering the circumstances.

As evening approached there seemed to be somewhat more order aboard *Carpathia*. Everyone was confined to their own areas in terms of class once again, but the atmosphere and treatment from the staff and passengers made us all feel as one. We had experienced such tragedy and now it was time to count our blessings and somehow find a way to move forward. I thought a lot about the time on board the *Titanic* and all I had experienced. I thought of the time spent with George and all he showed me. There were moments when I was envious of those in First Class and the luxury that they experienced during the voyage, yet all of that didn't seem to matter now.

Thinking about the possessions I left aboard the *Titanic*, I realized material possessions meant nothing as opposed to being with those I cherished most. Watching those who learned they had lost loved ones hurt not only my heart, but my soul. I couldn't begin to image what life would be like if I had lost Robert. I also began to really value my friendships and pledged to reach out to those I had lost contact with, especially those from my homeland. Moving to America five years ago was a very big decision for me, mostly because I felt I was missing out on all the world had to offer. And if I could somehow make it in America, I felt I would have more in my life. I somehow forgot or neglected all that I had left back in Ireland.

That first day aboard the *Carpathia* was one I spent mostly in deep thought. I couldn't help but to recollect the memories of my life to that point. Everything I had experienced and especially all that I witnessed in the last day. I thought of my book and wished I had one with me now so that I could lose myself in its pages. I wanted to read, yet my eyes were so tired and so stricken by what I had witnessed I couldn't concentrate. Every time I closed my eyes I saw images I wished to release. Helen and James held one another close and promised that they would make the best of the new life that awaited them, and that they would never take anything for granted.

When it came time for supper, we spoke with those sitting closest to us on the deck. We shared stories of where we each came from and where we were headed. We tried to comfort those who had lost loved ones and assured them they were in a better place now and out of pain, and that somehow they would always be looking over them. The children seemed to find that comforting even if their eyes stung with tears like their mother's eyes. I thought of young Charlie and how scared he must have been, but also knew that he was surrounded by love from his mother and siblings and that they would all be together again in heaven.

It was nearing 8:30 pm when my eyes began to close. Wrapped in blankets to stay warm, I fell into a deep sleep as my body's stress faded away. I would stay that way for a few hours, escaping to dreams and then suddenly be woken by a sound on deck that would bring me back to reality. By midnight all was quiet, the sky was pitch black, and lit by a thousand stars. Somehow I managed to fall asleep again and assured myself that tomorrow was a new day and everything would be okay.

CHAPTER 12

Day two aboard the *Carpathia* began with a beautiful sunrise. It served as a beacon of hope in my eyes that the worst was behind us and what awaited us in New York would somehow lessen the sting of the tragic events that had unfolded aboard the *Titanic*. I knew I had to remain strong, not just for my own sake, but for those around me. It was difficult at times, especially when met with eyes of those who clearly remained in a state of shock from the experience. I rose with a very stiff body. My back hurt but I knew I needed to provide my body with some movement, even if it just meant a short stroll around the deck. My legs were weak at first, but slowly the circulation began to flow and I felt a little more comfortable.

It was during my stroll that I found George.

"Good morning!" he greeted me with a smile on his face.

"Good morning George. Did you get any sleep?"

He smiled and shook his head side to side.

"You must be exhausted."

He motioned for me to sit and then signaled with his index finger that he would return. He came back with some warm bread and tea.

"Thank you."

He sat down next to me and ate some of the bread as well. We had a chance to catch up on what had taken place for each other over the last day. I asked him to tell me about his life back in England and what it was like for him growing up, and he was happy to share his story.

He came from a family of seamen from Southampton. His father was a dock laborer and George was the oldest of ten children. He had followed in his father's footsteps as loved the sea. Prior to his work on the *Titanic*, he worked on her sister ship, the RMS *Olympic* which was another transatlantic ocean liner. She was launched last year and made the same trip as the *Titanic* from Southampton, England to New York City, USA. He was excited about being on the maiden voyage of the *Titanic* as it had been highly publicized as the greatest ship ever built. He said he couldn't imagine anything of substance happening to such a ship as we had experienced, yet the great *Titanic* ultimately met its fate after striking the iceberg.

When I asked what he would do once we arrived in New York, he stated he would head back to Southampton to continue his work. He knew despite what had happened aboard the *Titanic*, that this was his life and one he had chosen. He knew it would be difficult returning home as many of the crew lived in Southampton and so many did not survive. He did say he felt grateful for his large family and knew they would not only be there for him when he returned, but would also look after those who lost loved ones.

Curious, I asked him if he had ever dreamt of leaving England and settling in America or any place else. He said he always dreamt of perhaps going to California and settling there for some time, but knew wherever he went it would be near the sea. He loved it and loved to swim. We shared that in common, although I'm not sure I could return to the sea after this experience, at least not straight away. He spoke of the sea with such praise and respect, how in any given moment its peacefulness and beauty could shift to sheer power and strength.

We spoke of those aboard the *Titanic* and what their lives must have been like, especially those in First

Class who seemingly were without a care in the world, compared to those in steerage who were just looking for a better life. He mentioned the many influential people who had been on board like Dorothy Gibson, a twenty-eight year old silent screen actress, and the Countess of Rothes, a well-known member of the British aristocracy who was on her way to America to meet her husband. John Jacob Astor, one of the world's richest men, estimated to be worth $150 million, and his wife had been returning from their honeymoon. Certainly they were housed in one of the suites on Millionaire's Row that we had passed on one of our adventurous tours.

We conversed for nearly an hour at which time he rose to leave.

"I must make rounds and see if my services are needed. I shall look for you after dinner and perhaps we can continue our conversation. I very much enjoy your company, Bridget."

I smiled and nodded my head in agreement. As he rose I caught a glimpse of his bright blue eyes and noticed something different. They lacked the light that once shown so bright. It was certainly understandable considering everything he had been through, yet it made me sad.

The afternoon brought with it gray clouds and word a storm was approaching, and that rain would follow in the evening. I found Helen and James in one of the general rooms for our class. They were conversing with another young couple that had miraculously survived.

"This is John and Mary. John was on the same collapsible boat with me and Mary on Lifeboat Six. They were very lucky."

John went on to explain how he had to wait with the other men and came across James on deck, and how they both jumped at the same time and managed to climb aboard the collapsible boat.

After dinner I returned to the General Room with Helen and James and we once again struck up a conversation with the other passengers. Before long George approached and said hello. I introduced him to the others as a member of the crew and our life saver.

"Care to join us George?" asked James.

"I'd be curious to know more about your view of the *Titanic* as a member of the crew. I'm sure you can share so much more than what we saw while aboard."

George smiled and sat down.

"What would you like to know?" he asked.

"I'd be curious to know what it was like in Southampton at the beginning of the route and during the other stops. Was there much fanfare?" replied James.

George straightened his body in the chair in preparation for what we anticipated would be a long story, yet one we were anxious to hear.

"I came aboard just after sunrise last Wednesday in Southampton. That's where I'm from. Prior to working on the *Titanic*, I worked on her sister ship, the *Olympic*, so I was familiar with the routine. Yet, I too was excited about her maiden voyage. Many of the crew had spent the night on the *Titanic*, those not from the area, yet I was able to sleep in my own bed the night before which was nice. Most of the passengers who boarded on the first day came from London and arrived on boat trains from Waterloo Station. These trains delivered them straight to White Star's dock.

There wasn't much fanfare and no special ceremonies planned. I did hear that the ship's musicians played on one of the upper decks, but I didn't witness this happening. I suppose the crowds cheered from both the decks and docks as they did with the *Olympic's* maiden voyage. That's usually customary. I did hear a few members of the engine crew missed the boat as they'd gone ashore to one of the pubs and lost track of time. Suppose they were the lucky ones in the end, huh." We each nodded in agreement at that statement.

"Were there any surprises or did anything of significance happen while leaving Southampton?" asked James.

"Well, can't say it really mattered in the long run, but we nearly collided with another ship while leaving port."

We all raised our eyebrows with curiosity.

"You don't say," stated James.

"Well, the channel where the *Titanic* needed to maneuver through to exit was very narrow. As we glided along we passed two other ships, the *Oceanic* and the *New York*. The powerful force of the *Titanic* passing caused the *New York* to snap her mooring ropes and swing out towards our ship. Somehow we passed unscathed, but it was close. We were only a few feet away when the order of Full Stern came down and the sudden blast of the *Titanic's* port propeller helped push the other ship away. It was then that the tugboats that were helping us maneuver out went back to help the *New York* moor elsewhere."

I sat there in amazement listening to George share his story. It seemed the *Titanic* had literally been making waves from the start. We never knew anything of this as the passengers we conversed with had all embarked in Queenstown as had we.

George then rose and excused himself.

"I'm sorry, but I need to make rounds again to see where I'm needed."

We all smiled and thanked him for telling us that story.

"Wow! I can only imagine what other stories he has to share," I thought.

"Perhaps we will meet again and I can ask him."

As my friends sat there conversing I thought about this man who had come into my life, and everything we had experienced in such a short time. I was devoted to Robert and had no plans to deter from my initial plan of returning to New York and building a life together. Yet there was a part of me that was so intrigued by George that I wondered where life would have taken us had we met in another time and place, and under different circumstances.

As evening approached the storm clouds began to move in and the smell of rain was in the air. My body was tired and I decided to return to my make-shift bed on the Promenade Deck. I wrapped my body in the blanket and lay down to rest. Before long I had drifted off into a deep sleep. I woke briefly to the rumble of thunder in the air, but managed to keep my eyes closed. Just then a bright flash of light lit up the sky that forced me to open my eyes. Then an explosion of thunder filled my body with terror. All of the sudden I was taken back to the *Titanic* and the nightmare we had experienced two night's prior. I sat up on the bed and my entire body was shaking. I grabbed the blanket and buried my face in it to close out the sound. It didn't help.

As I sat there with the blanket over my head I could hear the sounds of people mumbling and babies crying. They must have been startled by the storm as well. Some of the women were also crying and became somewhat hysterical with every flash of lightning and clap of thunder. I then spotted some of the stewards walking around trying to calm people down. I looked for George, but did not see him. How I wished he were here. I held onto the cross around my neck and just prayed we would survive. We were halfway to New York and I feared another disaster. I thought of

George's story about the ship, the *New York,* and wondered if perhaps it was an omen being so close yet not touching. Perhaps we weren't meant to reach the great city.

After several moments had passed, I tried to lie back down and fall asleep, yet it was impossible. My body continued to shake, my eyes had filled with tears, and I was truly terrified. Just then George found me.

"Are you okay?" he asked.

"Just shaken a bit," I replied, the tears burning my eyes.

"Close your eyes and I'll sit with you until you fall asleep. Don't worry, Bridget. I won't let anything happen to you. I promise."

I smiled and pulled the blanket up close to my face. He sat on the floor of the deck next to me and remained there until I fell asleep.

When morning arrived it was still overcast, but the storms has subsided a bit. I rose and headed into the General Room where I found Helen and James.

"We didn't want to wake you," said Helen as I entered.

I smiled and thanked her for her thoughtfulness.

It was a rough night, but George's words were encouraging and I knew everything would be alright.

Our third day aboard the ship was uneventful. I tried to rest my body as much as possible so that I could regain my full strength for when we arrived in America. I thought of George's comforting words and was grateful for his companionship. I was also grateful for Helen and James, but understood that they needed to have time alone as well. I also craved solitude at times. It was a time for reflection, a time of anticipation for the new life that awaited me in New York.

I thought of how quickly my life could have been disrupted had the circumstances aboard the *Titanic* been different. What if George hadn't reached us in time? What if we had been forced to stay behind on the ship as many others were? What would become of Robert when he learned the news? So many thoughts filled my mind that I was overwhelmed at times. The moments of solitude allowed the time and space for me to properly process everything that had taken place, to thank God for looking after us, and for sending George precisely when we needed him.

CHAPTER 13

RMS *Carpathia*
April 18, 1912

The rain had returned as we woke to greet our final day aboard the *Carpathia*, yet I didn't mind. We were one day closer to arriving in New York and I was ready to step foot on solid ground once again.

"How are you feeling this morning?" asked Helen.

"Better, thank you. I simply need to continue resting as much as possible. I'm not sure how I would have slept the last couple of evenings if it weren't for George. The storms gave me quite a fright."

"Yes, I know what you mean. The crying was the worst part. I tried to cover my ears, but it didn't seem to help much," replied Helen.

"Have you seen George yet this morning?" I asked.

"No. You two seem to be spending quite a bit of time together. Have you told him about Robert?"

"No. I tried to, but he always seems to interrupt me. He's sweet and I'm sure he means no harm. I'm just grateful he was there when we needed him, otherwise we wouldn't be having this conversation."

Helen and James both smiled in agreement. "Yes, he's certainly our hero in that respect," replied Helen.

"I'll tell him you said so as soon as I see him. He needs to know Robert will be greeting me when we reach New York. I'm sure he's probably terrified having most likely heard the news by this point. You know how he worries."

"Yes, I'm sure, but Robert also is quite aware of your sense of adventure and I'm sure he was relieved to receive the wireless from James. He knows by now that you have survived and have grand stories to tell," added Helen.

I gave her a stern look. "Well, it's certainly not the kind of story I was hoping to share about this voyage."

After breakfast we parted ways and I decided to head to one of the libraries on board the ship that had been used to house some of the passengers from the *Titanic*. I thought with one day left I could possibly find a nice book to read for the remainder of the journey, and rest my body in the process. As I was approaching the library I noticed George walking towards me down the promenade.

"Good morning, Miss Bridget. Did you manage to sleep well last night?" he asked.

"I did, thanks to you," I replied. "You've been so sweet staying next to me on the deck the last two nights. I appreciate that so much."

He smiled, tilted his head downwards and motioned with his right hand towards the ground. "Happy to be of assistance."

"How about you? Have you been sleeping well?"

"Oh yes. I'm used to all kinds of conditions aboard ship from my years on the sea. I feel as though I was born with sea legs and nothing seems to faze me."

I smiled and nodded my head in agreement. "Now that I can imagine," I replied.

"Where are you off to this morning?" he asked.

"The library. I thought perhaps I could find a book to lose myself in for the remainder of the voyage."

"Well, as luck would have it, I just came from the library and found a book I thought you might enjoy. I was hoping to run into you."

"Oh?" I asked as he handed over a thick red leather bound volume with gold lettering on it.

I took the book into my hands and read the title, *The Phantom of the Opera* by Gaston Leroux.

"Apparently it was originally released a few years back in French and this is the English version that was published last year."

"Oh, thank you George. I'm sure I will enjoy it."

He smiled, looking pleased with his decision to think of me and bring me the book.

"So how about you George? Where are you off to?"

"Oh, it's just another normal day for this sailor. Making sure all of our passengers are well and serve them if they should have any needs."

"You're such a good man, George. I'm sure White Star Line will reward you with a sterling accommodation for all you have done."

George laughed and replied, "Oh, no need. I'm simply doing my job."

"Oh George," I said hesitantly.

"Yes Miss?" he responded, looking straight at me.

"Would you have some time later today to talk? There is something I really feel I need to share with you before we arrive in New York. I know you have your duties to attend to, but I would appreciate a few moments of your time."

"Oh yes, Miss. I will have some time prior to supper if that would be alright?"

"That would be wonderful. I shall be in the library for most of the day, so you will probably find me there."

"I look forward to then, Miss," he said as he smiled and headed off.

When I arrived in the library I found it nearly empty, except for a few poor souls who appeared to be too weak to move. I headed towards an empty lounge chair near one of the book cases and found an older woman laying on a makeshift bed.

"Is it okay if I sit here to read?" I asked. "I promise not to disturb you."

"Oh yes, dear. That will be fine. I'm just resting. You will not disturb me," replied the woman in almost a whisper.

"Thank you," I replied as I sat down and rested the book on my lap. I took a moment to observe my surroundings, the quiet peaceful sense of the room as the rain continued to fall outside. I felt safe and happy to be surrounded by the beautiful volumes. I thought of Robert and the days that awaited us once I arrived back in New York. I was excited about our future.

Yet as I opened the book, I also thought of George, this kind man who had been so wonderful to me since we first met. I felt so comfortable being around him and we got along splendidly, yet I knew we must part ways once we reached New York. It was so sweet of him to think of me and find me this book to read for the remainder of the journey. I slowly turned the pages and became intrigued with the words I was reading.

"As it was true. For several months, there had been nothing discussed at the Opera but this ghost in dress-clothes who stalked about the building, from top to bottom, like a shadow, who spoke to nobody, to whom nobody dared speak and who vanished as soon as he was seen, no one knowing how or where."

I chuckled softly to myself thinking of George and how young Charlie called him the "magic man." This ghost sounded quite familiar and I had to wonder if perhaps this was where George got his inspiration for being quite incognito.

The time sped by as I found myself lost in the pages of this intriguing novel. Suddenly I heard movement about the room and promenade and realized it was time for dinner. I closed the book and headed back to the Saloon to meet Helen and James. They were waiting at a table when I arrived.

"Did you find a good book to read in the library?" asked Helen.

"Oh yes. Actually I found George and he gave me this volume," I replied showing them both the red book in my hand.

The Phantom of the Opera. "Sounds mysterious," said James as he leaned forward to take a closer look at the volume.

"It's fascinating actually. It's about this ghost at an Opera house in Paris. I can't wait to get back to it."

We had a lovely meal and spoke of our excitement upon reaching New York before the day was done.

Helen leaned over and whispered, "Did you tell George about Robert?"

"Not yet, but we are meeting prior to supper and I

will tell him then."

"Good."

After our meal I returned to the library as Helen and James decided to head to the General Room. They had found and befriended a small group of steerage passengers from *Titanic* and enjoyed sharing stories of their hopes once we all reached America. I found my same seat in the lounge chair and the women lying next to it seemed pleased to see me return. I smiled at her as I sat down and opened to the page where I had left off.

As the time passed I found myself lost in the storyline of the ghost, yet also nervously anticipating my conversation with George. He was so sweet and he seemed rather taken with me. I just hoped his feelings were those of friendship and not something more. I didn't want to disappoint him, yet I knew there was that risk. I was so grateful to have met him, to have had him rescue us and guide us to the lifeboat, and to be here aboard the *Carpathia* when I needed him. I had hoped there would be a way that we could remain in touch, yet knew that probably wouldn't be the case as we would return to lives that were already destined.

Sometimes I wondered if perhaps we had met in a different time and place what might have happened between us. We shared so much in common: the love of the sea, reading, travel, our spontaneous nature. I'm sure we could have been magnificent friends. I loved his sense of humor and how he always found a way to make me laugh, even in the most trying of times. I always felt safe around him and comfortable during our conversations. I knew that wherever life would take me, I would not forget him. I owed him my life.

Just then I looked up to find him standing before me.

"Hello Miss. Are you enjoying the book?"

"Immensely! Thank you so much."

"Shall we go for a stroll?"

"Yes, I would like that," I replied.

I placed my hand in his and stood to follow him.

"So in just a couple hours we will be docking in New York. I heard we were scheduled to arrive at 8:00 pm, although it will take some time to disembark. I'm sure they need to unload all of *Titanic's* lifeboats and then the passengers will be able to leave, but certainly in order by class, as is tradition."

"Oh, I see."

We continued to walk and our eyes would meet to which we would share a slight smile. He then stopped and placed both of his hands on each of my arms.

"Miss Bridget. I know we've only known one another for a short time, but I've become quite fond of you."

He then reached into the pocket of his jacket to pull something out.

"George wait. There's something I need to tell you."

Before I could utter another word, he opened his right hand to reveal the blue heart-shaped necklace we had observed on the beautiful woman at the party aboard *Titanic*.

"Oh my word. But how?" I asked.

"I spotted it wrapped around a piece of wood while we were in the lifeboat. I looked around the boat to see if I could spot the woman from the party, but she wasn't in our boat. I have been looking for her everywhere the last few days during my rounds, but have yet to locate her. She must have gone down with the ship. I thought of holding on to it and possibly trying to find a relative of hers once we reach New

York, but what are the odds?"

I stared at the necklace and didn't know what to say. It was even more stunning up close and I wanted so much to hold it, yet feared to touch it imagining the fate of its owner.

"I want you to have it Miss Bridget, as a reminder of my love for you. No matter where life takes us, know that you are always in my heart."

He took the necklace from his hand and placed it in mine wrapping my fingers around it. My eyes filled with tears of emotions I wasn't expecting.

"Please don't cry, Bridget."

I opened my left hand and looked at the necklace, the tears continuing to flow down my face. I then took George's hand as his expression changed to one of confusion. I placed the necklace back in his hand.

"Oh George. I cannot accept such a beautiful gesture. That is what I have been trying to tell you. I am promised to another man. His name is Robert and he awaits me in New York. We are to be married in August."

The look in George's eyes pierced my heart. There was so much sadness and pain in them. I wanted so much to take back the words, but I couldn't. It was the truth and I knew even though we had experienced so much together, and I wouldn't be alive if it weren't for him, we simply couldn't be together. Our lives had been predetermined and we needed to follow through with the paths that had been destined for us, regardless of how much it hurt in that moment.

I reached out to take hold of his arm, but he pulled back with his face turned towards the ground.

"I'm sorry to have bothered you Miss. I've been a fool. Please have a safe journey and I wish you well," he quietly said as he backed away.

"George wait!"

As I reached for him he turned and walked away. Suddenly the flow of people hid him from my view as the supper bell had rung. I stood there for a moment trying to digest what had just taken place. I knew it would be hard, but I didn't expect to feel the way I did, a feeling of regret. I loved Robert and I knew we would have a wonderful life together, but I had developed feelings for George and I didn't know quite how to acknowledge them.

I returned to the Saloon to find Helen and James at one of the tables. I had tried to wipe the tears from my eyes, but they were red and bloodshot. Helen noticed straight away.

"Are you alright? You've been crying," she asked.

"Yes, I'm alright. I told George about Robert and it was more difficult than I anticipated. I didn't realize his feelings towards me and I'm afraid I've hurt him dearly."

"Oh, I'm so sorry Bridget, but you know you had to. You and Robert are meant for one another. We've all known that for some time, and you two have a wonderful life ahead of you."

"I know. It was just difficult. George was so sweet and you and I both know we wouldn't be here if it weren't for him."

"Yes, I suppose you are right. Well, just be grateful for the time that you had together and hope that he's able to live a long happy life."

"Yes, I hope so."

By the time we finished our meal we were close to docking in New York. We gathered what little belongings we had and headed to the promenade to receive instruction about disembarking. As George had mentioned, the *Carpathia* first stopped opposite the

White Star pier to deposit the lifeboats retrieved from the *Titanic*. They were lowered into the harbor and each one was rowed to the pier by two *Titanic* crew members. I looked for George amongst them, but could not see him.

It appeared as though a large crowd of thousands had gathered on the pier and the ship was surrounded by dozens of yachts and other boats, some loaded with reporters who shouted questions through megaphones as flashes from their cameras lit up the sky. James had been able to send a wireless message to Robert while aboard the *Carpathia* assuring him that he along with Helen and I were all safe, so we knew he would be there to greet us.

It was nearly midnight before we finally left the ship. I never did find George.

CHAPTER 14

Lily

Coronado, California
April 15, 2012

As I sat on my bed contemplating the possibility of my dream's significance being a memory, I thought back to my life in general and my fears of the sea from such a young age. Perhaps it was all tied together somehow? Maybe my fears stemmed from another time, another place, a moment in time I was now beginning to recollect? I wasn't tired after such an eventful day and my mind seemed to be racing with more questions than answers.

I looked down at my phone and the time read 4:15 am. I knew I wouldn't be able to sleep and I was anxious to find answers to all the questions I had. I decided I would head to the beach and try to find the S.S. *Monte Carlo*. The forecasted negative low tide should reveal something for sure, I thought, or at least I hoped. I grabbed a small bag I could strap around my shoulders and put my phone, camera, and small flashlight in it. I threw on a sweat jacket, my rubber-soled beach shoes, and headed out.

The streets were fairly quiet as I headed up Orange Avenue. I arrived at the Hotel del Coronado and followed the pathway towards the beach. From there I headed south towards what has come to be known as Shipwreck Beach. There was some light from the Shores condominium complexes, but little near the sea. I took out my small flashlight from my bag and headed out onto the sand. As I made my way down the stairs from the walkway, I looked around but saw no one. It was an eerie feeling, yet I was curious to see what I would discover. The only sound was the crashing of the waves as I grew closer to the wreck. I aimed the flashlight towards the water and that is when I saw it, the magnificent vessel, or should I saw what remained of the S.S. *Monte Carlo*, sticking out of the sand.

At first I slowly moved my right arm to flash the light around the vessel. There were large pieces exposed and holes which I guessed had been windows or port holes of some kind. I managed to walk onto one of the larger exposed areas and felt this rush of energy go through me as if I had stepped back in time somehow. I didn't really know much about the ship, only that it was one of the gambling ships that had been anchored off the shores of Los Angeles County in the 1930s before it moved down to Coronado.

As I stood there I looked around me in awe of such a vessel, and imagined the stories it held that went down with the ship. I thought of everything I had experienced over the last week with the *Titanic* Centennial celebration and especially everything that happened last night. I removed the bag from my shoulders and got out my camera, and started taking photos so that I could capture the images before me. I slowly moved around from the larger area to a smaller landing closer to shore. I wanted to try to capture as many angles of the vessel as I possibly could.

Just then my eye caught sight of a flash of some kind. I moved in the direction from which is came and noticed the waves were also moving in a new direction and with greater force. I put the camera back into my bag and retrieved the flashlight once again. As I moved closer to where I had first noticed the flash, I seemed to lose track of where it had come from. I continued to move from the sand to pieces of the exposed vessel when my flashlight again caught a flash of blue. I needed to move closer, yet I felt restricted with the bag on my back. I took it off and flung it toward the beach so that was a far enough distance to not be exposed to the water.

I then returned to the spot where I had noticed the blue flash. I tried to focus the flashlight on the place I had seen the flash, but could not spot it. The waves were beginning to cover the smaller areas of the ship and the tide seemed to be shifting as I searched. Just then I saw it: a beautiful blue heart glistening from the light of my flashlight. I moved closer, trying to watch my step as well as keep an eye on the object. As I grew closer it appeared to be a stone of some kind, attached to a silver chain.

Stooping down to get a closer look I moved the flashlight from my right to my left hand so that I could reach for the object. The waves had become more and more intense and I was afraid it would wash away before I could grab it. There was a large gap between the small piece of exposed vessel where I stood and the piece where the stone hung. I squatted down as the waves crashed against my legs. I leaned forward to take hold of the stone.

"HEY YOU! BE CAREFUL!" shouted a voice from the shore.

At the moment I looked up to see who it was, a large wave came crashing against me, and the force knocked me into the water. Suddenly everything went black.

"Lily! Lily! Wake up. Please wake up! HELP! HELP! Someone help us!"

"I'm here. I hear you. What's happening? Why can't you hear me?"

I could hear voices and noticed lights around me. Suddenly some people were surrounding me. It was if I was viewing everything from above.

"What happened? Is she okay?"

"Call 911, we need help. YOU! Come here and cushion her head with this towel. She has a nasty cut. Keep her steady. I'm starting CPR."

I could see what was happening but felt helpless. It was David and he was kneeling over top of me, an expression of panic on his face, his blue eyes focused directly on me.

"David! What's happening? I'm scared."

"She's not breathing! Come on Lily, please, breathe, BREATHE!"

"I've got 911 on the line."

"GIVE ME THE PHONE! Yes, unconscious female, twenty-five, contusion to the right side of head, not breathing, performing CPR. On the beach at the foot of Avenida de las Arenas, Coronado.

"Ambulance is on the way." YOU THERE! Go to the parking lot and wait for the ambulance then show them where we are.

"RIGHT!"

I could see everything around me, the frantic state of the people moving about me, and David next to my side. I wanted so much to tell him I was okay, but he couldn't hear me.

"DAVID! QRF is here. What's happening?

"Matt! Thank God. It's my friend Lily. She was out by the *Monte Carlo* and a wave knocked her over. She must have hit her head as she has a nasty gash on the right side there. I went in after her but I could hardly see. She has a pulse now, but it's been touch and go. The ambulance is on the way."

"Okay, well we'll take it from here and support the paramedics when they get here. Why don't you get this crowd back and make sure there's space to move her?"

"I don't want to leave her."

"Hey pal, we've got this, and don't worry, she's in good hands. You know that."

I could see David moving away and a man I didn't recognize kneel down beside me. He removed the towel that had been placed on my head and proceeded to bandage the wound. He then placed a blanket on top of my body and motioned for the paramedics when they arrived. They placed me on a stretcher and took me to the ambulance that was parked in the lot between the condominium towers.

"David!"

"Hey Cap!"

"Mind telling us what happened here?"

"Sure thing Captain, umm, just give me a sec."

I noticed David running towards the ambulance, but a man stopped him.

"Hey, don't worry pal. We're taking her to SHARP. I'm sure the Captain will want the details and you'll have to fill out a report and all. She'll be fine, I promise you."

"Thanks Matt. I owe you."

A few hours had passed when I opened my eyes to view my surroundings. I was in a hospital room and the light hurt my eyes. I could hear voices from outside the room.

"Doctor! How is she?"

"She'll be okay with some rest David. She took a nasty blow and we want to monitor that head wound. She's been in and out of consciousness, so we're definitely keeping her overnight and will continue to monitor her."

"Can I see her?"

"Just for a few moments. She may not be awake."

"Thanks Doc."

I could hear the door open, but the strain of the lights forced my eyes to remain closed. I felt so tired and just wanted to sleep, yet I wanted to see David. I heard him pull up a chair close to the bed and he took my right hand in his.

"Oh Lily. You scared me to death."

"I'm sorry," I whispered.

"Lily! You're awake."

"Yes, but the light hurts my eyes. Is it okay if I just keep them closed?"

"Oh yes, of course. I won't stay long. I'm just so happy to know you're going to be okay. At least that's what Doc says. He does want to keep you overnight to monitor that bump on your head. Is there anyone you want me to call for you, your folks maybe?"

"Oh no, please don't bother them with this. I feel so foolish. I should have known better than to visit that silly ship at that crazy hour."

"Well, I'm the one who feels bad. I should have never shouted out at you, but I noticed the wave and, well, I'm sorry."

"Oh God, it's not your fault. I'm just happy you were there. You pretty much saved my life you know?"

"Well, I wouldn't go that far."

I opened my eyes slightly to see his face blush slightly and his blue eyes sparkle as they met mine.

"I'm so glad you're here David. I'm really tired though and want to sleep. Promise me you'll come back again?"

"Absolutely! After my shift, I promise."

"Thank you."

He then left the room and I fell into a deep sleep.

The following morning I woke with a nasty

headache and found the doctor in the room speaking to one of the nurses.

"Oh she's awake. Good morning Lily. How are you feeling this morning?"

"Well, I feel like I've been hit over the head with a two by four," I replied placing both hands on my head.

"Well, that's no surprise as you took one nasty blow to your noggin. I was going to release you today as the tests all came back okay, although I don't feel you should be alone. Do you have family or someone who can look after you for the next few days?"

"Umm, well no. I live…."

"No worries Doc, I'll take care of her," interrupted David as he walked in the door.

"Good morning Sunshine!" he said as he approached the bed and whipped out a beautiful bouquet of purple tulips from behind his back.

"Oh David, they are beautiful, but you shouldn't have, and I can't ask you to look after me."

"Shhh now Lily. I am a trained public servant and here to assist."

"Well, there you go," replied the doctor. "I'll be

back shortly with your release papers."

After he and the nurse left the room, David pulled up a chair next to the bed and took my hand.

"Look Lily, at least let me do this for you. It'll make me feel better and it's nothing really."

"But what about your work?"

"No worries there. I swapped shifts with my buddy Matt and I'm all yours for the next two days."

CHAPTER 15

Coronado, California
April 16, 2012

A short while later the doctor returned with the release papers and David helped me to a wheelchair which was standard procedure when exiting after a night's stay at the hospital.

"I could just roll you home since we're only a couple blocks away, you know," he said.

"HA! I'm sure you don't want to add "Grand Theft Wheelchair" to your spotless record as a public servant, do you?" I replied.

"HAHA! Yeah, probably not a good idea. No worries. I'm just parked around the corner. Let's go."

When we arrived at the apartment I looked at David with a puzzled expression.

"Looking for these?" he said as he handed me my keys. "I found your bag on the beach with your camera, phone, and these."

"Oh man. WOW! Thanks. I had completely

forgotten about that."

"No worries," he replied as he held open the screen door so I could unlock the main one.

We entered the apartment and I put down my bag and went over the fridge to get a bottle of water as I felt dehydrated.

"Water?" I asked holding up a bottle.

"Sure, thanks!" he replied. "You have a really nice place here, Lily."

"Thank you. I like it. There's a guestroom that you're welcome to use so you don't have to sleep on the couch. I really do appreciate you looking after me and really want you to be comfortable."

"Thanks! I'm fine sleeping on the floor, but will happily take the guest bed," he replied with a smile on his face. "The doctor said you should try to get as much rest as you can over the next two days, but if you sleep during the day I have to make sure I wake you every two hours or so."

"Yeah, he mentioned that as well. No strenuous activities for a while, just take it easy."

"Yep! I actually brought you something. You mentioned how you love to read and write so I brought you a book. Hope you haven't read it. The title made me think of you."

"Oh?" I replied as he pulled the book from his bag.

As he placed it in my hand I noticed the title, *The Story Girl* by L.M. Montgomery.

"Oh wow! I love this author. She wrote the *Anne of Green Gables* series. I love her work, but I haven't read this one. Thank you so much."

"Phew! Good. I was worried you might have read it."

"No, I'm grateful. In fact, I have a bit of a silly confession. For a couple years I was crazy obsessed with the story of Anne. I once dreamt of becoming a figure skater and spent a summer training at a facility in Ontario. That year I actually managed to visit most of Canada and I even made it out to Prince Edward Island, to Cavendish, where the story takes place. I was able to visit the gabled house that inspired the story as well as the different settings from the books, including the Haunted Wood and Lover's Lane."

David laughed. "Lover's Lane huh?"

"I know it's silly now, but back then I thought it was the greatest thing ever, and I can't wait to read this story. Thanks again. You're the best."

"Aw shucks. Well thank you, kind lady," he

replied turning his head away.

"While you're reading, do you want me to put something together for lunch?"

"I'm afraid the fridge is pretty bare. I really should run to the market."

"Nonsense. I'll go."

"There's a list by the microwave. Let me get you some money."

"Don't worry about it. I'll put it on my card and you can just pay me back. No big deal. Anything in particular you would like for lunch?"

"You know, I'm actually craving Subway. Perhaps a six inch tuna on Italian?"

"Fabulous! Subway for lunch it is. Be back in a flash."

As the door closed I placed my bottle of water on the coffee table and grabbed a blanket from my bedroom. I then lay on the sofa and began to read. As my eyes followed the words along the page, my mind thought of David and how sweet he was to find me this book, and how funny that it was by one of my favorite authors. I smiled thinking of how attentive he was, how caring and considerate. I felt so happy to have made a new friend here on the island, as I hadn't expected to have experienced so much together over such a short period of time.

Before long David had returned with the groceries and our lunch.

"I'm back! Are you enjoying the book?"

"Oh yes, immensely. But I must confess to being a bit distracted thinking of all that has taken place over the last week."

David smiled and replied, "Quite the adventure huh?"

"No kidding!

I straightened up from the sofa and took a sip of water.

"Can I ask you something?

"Sure, shoot!" replied David.

"Well, what exactly happened out at the shipwreck? I remember being out by the wreck and taking photos. I remember noticing some sort of flash of light and wanting to get a closer look. Then it's pretty much all a blank until I woke up in the hospital."

"Well, it was pretty scary from my point of view to be honest. I saw you by the wreck. You were stooped down reaching for something when I spotted this large wave coming towards you. I shouted out, but it was too late. The wave hit you and you fell into the water. You must have hit your head on part of the vessel and the tide pulled you down into one of the holes alongside the wreck. I lost sight of you and ran in to help."

"Wow! I don't remember any of that."

"Yeah, it was scary. I had to be careful myself as you can get sucked into those holes pretty quickly, plus the water is so murky that you can't really see anything. I tried to feel my way alongside the vessel with one hand hoping to find you, while also protecting my head with the other so as to not come up on any sharp crevices. Luckily I was able to find you before too long and grab hold of your clothing and pull you up. I was grateful for the little bit of light we had by that point from daybreak. I was a little disoriented with where we were since the tide had shifted and completely covered the wreckage. Luckily I was able to make it back to shore in time."

"Wow! In a way I'm glad I don't remember. I would have been terrified. Thank God you were there and knew what to do."

"Well, I'm just happy you're okay," he replied as

he rubbed the side of my arm.

"Now how about some lunch?"

"Oh yes. I'm starved."

The rest of the day was pretty quiet. I read my new book and David worked on his laptop and checked in with Matt at work to make sure everything was going smoothly. I dozed off occasionally and he would wake me after a few hours. We had a lovely dinner which he prepared and by 8:30 pm I felt ready for bed. He kissed my forehead and wished me a good night.

"I'm just in the next room if you need anything, Lily."

"Thank you. Goodnight!"

The following morning I woke and the headache seemed to have subsided. The sensitivity to light no longer was problematic and I was beginning to feel like my old self again. I opened the door to my bedroom around 7:30 am and found the table set for breakfast and David in the kitchen standing over the stove fixing scrambled eggs.

"Morning, Sunshine!"

I smiled as I looked around the room. "You did all this? How long have you been awake?"

"Since 5:30 am. Already went for my run and ready for a new day. I looked in on you before I left and you seemed so peaceful in your sleep, I didn't want to disturb you."

"Wow! I didn't even hear you get up."

"That was the idea," he replied with a wink. "Please, sit down. This will be ready in no time."

He pulled out the chair for me to sit in and then poured some orange juice into the glass to the right of my plate.

"Hungry?"

"Yes, and it smells delicious."

"Well, we've got to get your energy back and fuel into your body. You know, you've been through a traumatic experience."

"Yes, doctor," I said with a slight smile.

"Hmm, Doctor James! Has a nice ring to it, don't you think?"

"Ha! Yes, it does," I replied.

He then approached the table and placed the plate before me. Scrambled eggs, two slices of wheat toast with cream cheese and strawberries, and two slices of crispy bacon.

"Oh yum! I can so get used to this."

"Haha! Well, glad you approve. I have to go back to work tomorrow, so figured I should at least make a good impression before I go," he replied with a big smile that spread from ear to ear.

"How's the head feel today?"

"Much better, thank you and the light doesn't seem to bother me anymore."

"Good. Sounds like you'll be back to yourself in no time."

"Yes!"

After breakfast I decided to rest on the sofa and write in my journal as David continued to work on his laptop.

I began to write –

April 17, 2012

I'm not sure where to start. The last week has been something straight out of a movie in some ways. I think back to everything that has happened and wonder if it was just a dream or did I actually experience it all. The move to Coronado Island was something I felt so strongly about doing when I was in Santa Monica, and now I'm beginning to feel there's just so much more to it. You see, I have met someone. His name is David. He's a local lifeguard and really sweet guy. We met on the beach last week as I was exploring the area around the shipwreck of the S.S. Monte Carlo which was a gambling ship from the 1930s. We ended up hitting it off and he invited me to attend this fancy dinner at Prado restaurant in Balboa Park in conjunction with the Centennial anniversary of the sinking of Titanic. It was an incredible event and I'd never seen, nor eaten so much food in one sitting in my life. David seemed to really enjoy the feast as well which made me laugh. I got to meet his parents who were both really nice and I had a lovely time.

The next morning I couldn't sleep and decided to head back out to the shipwreck as the tides were low enough that the wreckage would be visible. I was taking photos and then I thought I spotted something, a flash of light caught my eye. Yet when I got closer to see what it was, I was knocked into the water by a large wave. Luckily David was passing by on his morning run just in time to save me. Not sure what would have happened if he hadn't been there. Anyhow, I ended up in the hospital with a concussion and once released have been resting here at home. Thankfully, I'm under David's care as he insisted on looking after me for a couple days since the doctor didn't want me to be alone, simply as a precaution should there be any post-concussion symptoms.

David has been so sweet. He fixed me this amazing breakfast this morning and even went out and got lunch and groceries for us yesterday. He even bought me a book to read while I recovered and it's by one of my favorite authors, L.M. Montgomery. It's called The Story Girl and he said the title reminded him of me. So sweet. I'm really enjoying it and really love his company. I guess I'm just curious as to why I feel so comfortable around this man I hardly know. I felt it from the moment he said hello, as if I did know him somehow, although I can't remember from where. Perhaps it's just all in my head. My poor head. What a beating it has taken.

Anyhow, it's been an adventurous few days, that's for sure. I was curious to explore the significance of my dream when I came down here, and yet now I feel as though I have more questions, than answers. Suppose only time will tell.

As I sat there pen in hand, I closed the journal before me as David approached.

"Whatcha writing?"

"Oh, it's my journal. Just jotting down notes of the adventurous week we've had. Figured if I didn't get it down now, I might just forget."

"Not sure I could forget."

"Yeah, I know what you mean. It's been crazy, memorable if anything."

"Yeah."

"Hey, can I ask you something?" I asked

motioning for David to join me on the sofa.

"Shoot!"

"Well, you know when we were at the exhibit following dinner on Saturday night, and they were playing that song from *Titanic*?"

"Yeah."

"Well, what did you feel when you heard it? I know with me it sent chills up my spine. I can't really explain it."

"Yeah, it was the same for me. It was like all sorts of emotions rolled up into one. Anxiety, fear, sadness, relief. I thought I was going to get sick really. That's why I suggested we leave. Truth be told, I needed some air."

"Yeah, I understand. It was the same for me. Why do you think we reacted that way?"

"I don't know. I thought back to my dream and the images I saw, but more so the sounds I heard. The emotions I felt at the exhibit seemed to match what I feel when I think of the dream if that makes any sense."

"David?"

"Yes."

"I've been thinking. Have you ever considered that the dreams we've been having may be more than simply dreams?"

"How so?"

"Well, what if they are memories?"

"Memories of what?"

"Of another time, another place."

David looked at me with this intense look on his face, his blue eyes seemed brighter than I had ever noticed. He turned slowly and placed his hand on the cover of *The Story Girl* book that lie on the coffee table. He then took my hand and said softly.

"There's something I need to show you. I'm not sure if it means anything, but it's just a feeling I have."

He then rose from the sofa and went over to his lifeguard jacket that rested on the dining room chair. He lifted it from the chair and returned to the sofa. He unzipped one of the pockets and then paused.

"During my run this morning I decided to stop by the wreck. I'm not sure why. It was as if something drew me there. The sun was just coming up and I could see small pieces of the wreckage through the sand. There were many sea creatures that had nestled up again the wreck and I stooped down to get a closer look. The colors and shapes were beaming in the sunlight. That's when I saw it."

"Saw what?"

He retrieved an object from the pocket of his jacket and placed in it my hand. When I looked down I couldn't believe my eyes. It was a blue heart-shaped stone surrounded by diamonds with a diamond clip that hung on a thin silver chain. I sat there with my mouth half open, no words to express its beauty. I couldn't take my eyes off of the piece.

I closed my hand around the piece and simultaneously closed my eyes. Suddenly flashes from my dream began to fill my mind along with new images I hadn't yet experienced. I saw a man with the same blue eyes as David. I saw him place the necklace in my hand. I then saw what felt like myself, yet with a different face take the piece and put in back into the man's hand as my eyes filled with tears. Just then a single tear slowly made its way down my cheek.

"Are you okay?" asked David.

I opened my eyes to see the piercing blue of his looking back at me. I took his hands in my own and asked, "Is it you?"

To be continued

ACKNOWLEDGEMENTS

It's been quite the journey in writing this book, my first piece of historical fiction after seven non-fiction works. As a writer and artist I'm a big believer in growing in my craft and I've loved the process and challenge of creating a work of fiction. I have so many people to thank who have helped guide me through this process.

First of all, a big thank you to my best friend and partner, William who was my rock and helped in bringing out the character traits of the male leads in the book. This book would not exist without him.

I'd also like to thank my family who has been so supportive on this journey. To Tad Fitch who was such a big help in providing information on Bridget's life so that I could have a model and template to follow, my deepest thanks. I loved learning about her and everything she experienced. To Eve Thomas, my dear friend, many hugs as well as thanks. Having someone to share my passion for the history of *Titanic* was wonderful. To my fabulous friends and colleagues in Coronado, especially Ian Urtnowski who provided me with answers to the questions about the shipwreck and the tides, my hats off to them. To my fabulous friends and colleagues in Santa Monica who have been so supportive since I arrived in LA four years ago, please know I am so grateful for you all.

To my fabulous editor, Marlene Oulton, for your guidance and support on this beautiful journey of ours, many thanks. To the staff from the Natural History Museum in San Diego, the Titanic Historical Society, and the authors of the MANY books I read about the *Titanic* over the last two years in my research, thank you! Also, a very special thank you to fellow author, K.M Weiland, and those who write fiction for your guidance along the way. It helped immensely.

….and a special thanks to YOU, the reader for allowing me to open up my imagination and create this story for you. I hope you have enjoyed it and I hope we'll visit again in 2019 when the sequel, *SHUFFLING THE TIDES* is published.

Stay tuned. The adventure has only just begun.

ABOUT THE AUTHOR

Cali Gilbert is an international bestselling author, award winning photographer, social entrepreneur, and book coach. As a former figure skater and magazine publisher, with an extensive background in event management, Cali assisted the Canadian Olympic Committee at the 2002 Winter Olympic Games in Salt Lake City, Utah while supporting the staff at Canada House, and most recently served as an Event Ambassador for the 34th America's Cup sailing regatta in San Francisco in 2013.

In 2012 Cali created the *IT'S SIMPLY* series of books and has published several bestselling books of her own, and now supports other writers through her company, *Serendipity Publishing House*. Cali is also an inspirational speaker for women's groups and is currently working on new projects as a filmmaker to share her stories and message of hope with the world.

Cali is passionate about serving her community, inspiring women in transition to live in alignment with their purpose, and encouraging youth to reach their full potential. She splits her time between Santa Monica and Coronado Island, California.

WWW.CALIGILBERT.COM

Other books by Cali Gilbert

It's Simply...Sausalito: An Inspirational Journey
ISBN-13 978-1467924436
ISBN-10 1467924431

It's Simply...GOLDEN: 75 Years of Inspiration
ISBN-13 978-1467903615
ISBN-10 1467903612

It's Simply...SF: Our City by the Bay
ISBN-13 978-1469969282
ISBN-10 1469969289

It's Simply SAILING: Our Voyage to the 2013 America's
Cup
ISBN-13 978-1475108910
ISBN-10 1475108915

It's Simply Serendipity: Four Steps to Manifesting a Life of
Bliss
ISBN-13 978-1475195538
ISBN-10 1475195532

It's Simply Publishing: Step by Step Guide to Writing,
Marketing & Publishing Your First Book
ISBN-13 978-1497488274
ISBN-10 1497488273

PEARL: A Guide to Living an Authentic & Purposeful Life
ISBN-13 978-1503031098
ISBN-10 1503031098

48259676R00124

Made in the USA
San Bernardino, CA
21 April 2017